D0040475

TO THE DEATH

Fargo fired his last bullet, dropping one of the riders. He was pinned down.

Butch Robinson shouted, "Run up the white flag, Fargo! We'll take you in for a fair trial!"

"I'll run my boot up your ass!" Fargo yelled back.

"Make it hot for this mouthpiece, boys!" Butch shouted.

The crackling explosion of gunfire sounded like an ice floe breaking apart. *It's curtains*, Fargo told himself, though even now he felt no fear. He'd be damned if he was going to just hunker down and die like a pig at slaughter. He'd go out fighting his enemies and on his feet like a man.

Even as lead blurred the air around him, Fargo yanked the Arkansas Toothpick from its boot sheath and launched himself to his feet.

"Come on, then, you sniveling weak sisters!" he roared out with the powerful bray of a buffalo bull bellowing. "Skye Fargo never had plans to live forever!"

THE
TRAILSMAN

#281

NEW MEXICO
NIGHTMARE

by

Jon Sharpe

A SIGNET BOOK

SIGNET
Published by New American Library, a division of
Penguin Group (USA) Inc., 375 Hudson Street,
New York, New York 10014, USA
Penguin Group (Canada), 10 Alcorn Avenue, Toronto,
Ontario M4V 3B2, Canada (a division of Pearson Penguin Canada Inc.)
Penguin Books Ltd., 80 Strand, London WC2R 0RL, England
Penguin Ireland, 25 St. Stephen's Green, Dublin 2,
Ireland (a division of Penguin Books Ltd.)
Penguin Group (Australia), 250 Camberwell Road, Camberwell, Victoria 3124,
Australia (a division of Pearson Australia Group Pty. Ltd.)
Penguin Books India Pvt. Ltd., 11 Community Centre, Panchsheel Park,
New Delhi - 110 017, India
Penguin Group (NZ), cnr Airborne and Rosedale Roads, Albany,
Auckland 1310, New Zealand (a division of Pearson New Zealand Ltd.)
Penguin Books (South Africa) (Pty.) Ltd., 24 Sturdee Avenue,
Rosebank, Johannesburg 2196, South Africa

Penguin Books Ltd., Registered Offices:
80 Strand, London WC2R 0RL, England

First published by Signet, an imprint of New American Library,
a division of Penguin Group (USA) Inc.

First Printing, March 2005
10 9 8 7 6 5 4 3 2 1

The first chapter of this book previously appeared in *Texas Tart,* the two
hundred eightieth volume in this series.

Copyright © Penguin Group (USA) Inc., 2005
All rights reserved

REGISTERED TRADEMARK—MARCA REGISTRADA

Printed in the United States of America

Without limiting the rights under copyright reserved above, no part of this
publication may be reproduced, stored in or introduced into a retrieval system, or transmitted, in any form, or by any means (electronic, mechanical,
photocopying, recording, or otherwise), without the prior written permission
of both the copyright owner and the above publisher of this book.

PUBLISHER'S NOTE
This is a work of fiction. Names, characters, places, and incidents either are
the product of the author's imagination or are used fictitiously, and any resemblance to actual persons, living or dead, business establishments, events, or
locales is entirely coincidental.

If you purchased this book without a cover you should be aware that this
book is stolen property. It was reported as "unsold and destroyed" to the
publisher and neither the author nor the publisher has received any payment
for this "stripped book."

The scanning, uploading, and distribution of this book via the Internet or via
any other means without the permission of the publisher is illegal and punish-
able by law. Please purchase only authorized electronic editions, and do not
participate in or encourage electronic piracy of copyrighted materials. Your
support of the author's rights is appreciated.

The Trailsman

Beginnings . . . they bend the tree and they mark the man. Skye Fargo was born when he was eighteen. Terror was his midwife, vengeance his first cry. Killing spawned Skye Fargo, ruthless, cold-blooded murder. Out of the acrid smoke of gunpowder still hanging in the air, he rose, cried out a promise never forgotten.

The Trailsman they began to call him all across the West: searcher, scout, hunter, the man who could see where others only looked, his skills for hire but not his soul, the man who lived each day to the fullest, yet trailed each tomorrow. Skye Fargo, the Trailsman, the seeker who could take the wildness of a land and the wanting of a woman and make them his own.

Northern New Mexico Territory, 1859—
where the night itself can stalk a man,
turning the hunter into the hunted.

1

Bad dreams were nothing new to Elena Vargas. But usually they came while she was asleep.

It was broad daylight now, and the young Mexican woman was wide awake—and so terribly frightened that her heart pounded like fists on a drum.

"Por favor, señor," she was forced to whisper, her throat dry and constricted with terror. "Only a few doors down, you will see a cantina with red *farolitos* burning in the windows. Sometimes there are women there of— of the type you seek."

The metallic *snick,* when her tormentor thumbed back the hammer of his big pistol, was the loudest sound she'd ever heard.

"Shut your piehole, *puta.* Just peel them clothes off and get on that bed, or I'll decorate the walls with your brains."

His voice, like hers, was a whisper—but a harsh, forced, grating whisper. Somehow Elena didn't think it was deliberate whispering. Rather, something seemed wrong with his voice.

"Por favor," she repeated, lips trembling. "I have a little money, I could—"

"Damn you, woman, didn't I say shut *up*?"

With a snarl of rage the intruder ripped off her low-cut *camisola.* Elena had no idea who he was. She had been sitting at the table, sewing piecework, when the tall stranger whipped aside the Navajo blanket that covered her doorway.

Elena had glimpsed a fringed buckskin shirt, a dark beard, a shadowy face as flat and unreadable as a stone slab. But then he had quickly closed the window shutter before she got a better look at him.

Now that he knew she was too scared to scream, he jammed the big pistol into a bright scarlet sash around his waist. She shuddered violently when his big, rough hands began fondling her bare breasts.

No, not fondling—"attacking" was more accurate. There was no lust in his touch, only anger.

"Dirty dugs," she heard him mutter. "A pretty little Mexer hoor with big ol' dirty dugs. Sticking way out, and wiggling 'em when you walk so's a man'll get all het up."

She gasped when he tore her skirt off. Now Elena was naked, and he pushed her roughly onto the bed, fumbling open his trousers.

"Spread 'em, *puta*."

Puta . . . Elena was not a whore and never had been. Out of pride and piety, she had even refused to be respectfully "kept" by a mannerly Santa Fe lawyer who had a wife back East.

But she had been raped before and assumed she probably would be again. *Sabe Dios*—God knows—life was cruel and she was a young, pretty woman on her own. This was a lawless territory where evil men took what they liked without asking.

She closed her eyes and waited, praying it would be brief and that he would not hurt her afterward.

But nothing happened.

The stranger just stood there in the dimness beside the bed. She could hear his breath coming in short, ragged gasps.

A minute ticked slowly, torturously past, then two. The man stood as if bolted to the floor.

Then, incredibly, Elena thought she heard a sob wrenched from him.

"Señor?" she said hesitantly.

"You filthy little beaner harlot, I said *shut up*!"

Her heart leaped into her throat when the cold, huge bore of the pistol kissed her left temple.

Silently, Elena said a Hail Mary, preparing herself for death.

2

"Woman," rasped the odd, harsh whisper, "cross your legs and close the gates to hell!"

With that, the intruder lowered the hammer and shoved his weapon back into the sash. He moved to the doorway and stepped quickly past the blanket.

The glaring afternoon sunlight forced him to squint after the interior dimness. For a long moment he pressed flat against the girl's shack, carefully watching the sleepy little town.

Chico Springs, in northeastern New Mexico Territory, was still so rustic that the main—and only—street was hardly more than a rutted dirt path. In front of the livery, right next door, a yellow, flea-bitten cur glanced at the man briefly, then lazily licked itself. The hot, breezeless air was still and silent except for the drone of cicadas.

Otherwise, the flyblown town looked almost deserted. The only other person on the street was an old woman of mixed Yaqui and Mexican blood. She sat cross-legged before her mud hovel, grinding corn on a *metate*.

It was child's play to slip unseen between the livery and the shack. He hurried up a sandy slope behind the town. He'd tethered his blaze-faced sorrel in a thicket atop the slope.

When he thought he was safe, he felt the old, familiar sense of rage and shame filling him like a glass under a pump.

The same ugly feeling he had first felt, fifteen years earlier in St. Louis, when that smallpox-scarred whore had taunted him: *Hell, boy, you got a tallywhacker that don't whack. Can you at least pee with it?*

"It ain't nothing wrong with *me,* dammit," he said in his harsh whisper, startling his grazing horse. "Pa was right. It's them damn sluts. The devil can enter any of the seven holes in a woman's body, and *that* hole especially."

He poked his head out just enough to see the town below. Some of the buildings were dark brown adobe. But others—including the livery and the woman's shack next door—were made of wood.

Old, weathered boards sapped to pure tinder by the southwest sun.

3

His mood suddenly improved, and he felt a grin tugging at his lips. He still couldn't believe he was being so well paid to do the only thing he loved doing.

Again his eyes cut to the pretty woman's shack, the livery next door.

A livery stuffed with hay and straw. His new employer wouldn't have to pay him for this next job. It would be a labor of love.

Tonight! The night was his time, it was darkness and stillness that unleashed his awesome, manly power and might.

And with that thought came the physical arousal he had failed to achieve minutes ago.

Skye Fargo kneed his pinto stallion up out of a long cutbank, then drew rein. His slitted gaze swept the terrain to make sure it was safe to skyline himself. Then he stood up in the stirrups to ease the pressure on his saddle-sore tailbone.

He had finally reached the end of the Cimarron cutoff, the only northern route into New Mexico Territory that skirted rock-strewn Raton Pass. Due west, straight ahead of him, loomed the towering Sangre de Cristo range, with the Rio Grande valley tucked out of sight just behind them and Santa Fe a few days ride to the southwest.

It was vastly more lush and green here than in the desolate landscape farther south. This was rolling foothill country, the grassy slopes dotted with towering evergreens. Craggy-barked cottonwoods marked the banks of numerous creeks.

"Well, old campaigner, welcome to the land of Coronado," he remarked to the Ovaro. "We should make Chico Springs around sunset. Then we'll slap an oat bag on you."

Fargo's belly rumbled like an underground thermal spring. Hours earlier he'd gnawed the remainder of his last pemmican cake.

Before he rode on, Fargo drew his Colt. He spun the cylinder with a fast, rattling click like a roulette wheel, then gave a quick puff to clear blow sand out of the Colt's action. He leathered his weapon and slipped the

4

riding thong over the hammer. He quickly checked the magazine in his brass-framed Henry, then booted the rifle again.

A man was wise not to be lulled by the pretty vista around here. This was treacherous country where men were shot for their boots. This ancient land had been violent and dangerous long before General Kearny hoisted the U.S. flag over the territory of New Mexico.

Fargo shook the kinks out of his arms, then changed hands on the reins. As he nudged the Ovaro up to a fast trot, he especially watched the thickets, rock tumbles, and pockets of deep grass—all favored by ambushers.

He reached Chico Springs without incident just after sunset. The one-horse burg had begun as a campsite for wagon trains after they rounded Point of Rocks on the Santa Fe Trail. The only thing that had grown much, since Fargo's last visit, was the *camposanto*—the cemetery on the eastern edge of town.

As he rode in he could spot the flickering glow of *farolitos* through open doorways. There was no church, but anyplace where the walls were thick enough, niches held cheap plaster busts of beloved saints. Fargo reined in at the livery barn on the far side of town.

"Well, God a'mighty!" exclaimed the hostler when he got a good look at the Ovaro in the oily yellow glow of a kerosene lantern. "Son, that stallion is high-grade horseflesh."

The old codger was at least sixty, with a face marked by deep seams. But his twinkling eyes were alive with sly good humor.

Fargo was surprised when the Ovaro, usually wary around strangers, nuzzled the old man's bony shoulder. "Say . . . looks like you got a way with horses."

"I oughter. First forty years of my life, onliest time I clumb outta the saddle was to crap. The name's Hooky McGhee, and I use to break green horses to leather for the army. But there's cobwebs on them memories, boy."

"Rubdown and a feed," Fargo said, flipping the old-timer a four-bit piece.

Fargo nodded toward the open double doors. Across the street, an armed guard sat next to a stack of new boards. There were very few sawmills this far west, and huge freighting difficulties. Now lumber thieves were prowling the far frontier, where finished boards were at a premium.

"The board bandits have invaded this area, too?" Fargo asked.

"Huh! Does a rag doll have a patched ass?"

Fargo headed toward the center of town and the only cantina, whose owner had never bothered to hang out a sign. He stepped through a doorless archway into a dimly lighted, smoky room with an earthen floor.

A Pueblo Indian wrapped in a traditional *manta* was placing steaming bowls down in front of two Mexicans at one of the tables. A third customer nursed a bottle of tequila at a deal counter. The place was so primitive that the chairs were simply hardtack boxes and empty packing crates.

"Muy buenas tardes, señor," the Indian owner greeted him as Fargo parked himself at the far end of the counter, so he could face the doorway. "I am Antonio Two Moons, *a sus ordenes*—at your service."

The moon-faced owner squinted slightly, studying Fargo's face closer. "You have been here before, *verdad*? Perhaps . . . two years ago?"

Fargo nodded. "That's some memory you got, Antonio."

"No, I forget many faces. But not yours. You are the *gringo famoso*—the Trailsman."

"This *gringo* is more famished than famous."

The word "famished" confused Antonio. *"Tiene usted hambre, señor?"*

"Damn straight, I have hunger. Right now I'd eat a skunk."

"The only skunks around here, *señor*, walk on two legs, *verdad*? But I have hot beans and tortillas."

Fargo flipped four bits onto the counter. "Trot it out, *amigo*."

Antonio bit the small coin to make sure it was good. *" 'Sta bien, señor."*

The food was simple, but tasty and filling. Fargo washed it down with milky white *pulque,* the cactus liquor he preferred to tequila.

"Señor, will you be visiting Chico Springs long?" Antonio asked as he refilled Fargo's glass.

Fargo shook his head. "I'm pushing on to Fort Union. The post commander wants to hire me as a scout for a road-building crew."

Just as Fargo finished speaking, an Anglo male wearing a big buffalo-hide coat stepped into the cantina. Fargo was instantly alerted—he'd learned from experience never to trust any man who was dressed too warm for the weather.

The man was bearing right toward him. Fargo snapped his Colt out onto the counter, holding it but not cocking the hammer.

"Care to purchase a good firearm, friend?" Fargo called out in a hail-fellow tone. "It's well used, but also well oiled."

The new arrival froze in midstep, looking confused and uncertain. Then a cunning gleam seeped into his small, dull eyes. He flashed big buck teeth.

"Might could be I do need a short-iron. Lemme see it."

Fargo thumbed back the hammer. "I got a better idea. First you pull that hog-grinder out from under your coat. Butt-first and *slow,* or I'll blow you to hell."

The cantina went silent like a courtroom after a confession. Those crude chairs scuffed the rammed-earth floor as patrons cleared a lane.

"Sainted backsides!" Antonio Two Moons crossed himself. "Saint Joseph, pray for us," he muttered.

The man in the hide coat hesitated. Fargo wagged the Colt for emphasis. "Right damn now, mister."

Scowling, the man slowly drew a sawed-off scattergun out from under his coat and put it on the counter. Fargo noticed both hammers were cocked.

"I wasn't planning to kill you, mister," the man muttered. "Only to get the drop on you and turn you over to the law in Springer."

Fargo broke open the gun's breech, pocketed the shells, and flung the weapon aside. "Why? You don't like my face?"

"Why? Don't try to hornswoggle me, stranger. You're

7

tall, got a beard, and you're wearing buckskins. That's ex-*act*ly the description of the jasper that tried to rape Elena Vargas a few hours ago."

Fargo had no idea what the man meant, but he believed his story—this man did not have the look of a casual killer.

"Next time I see you, rapist," the man added, "it'll be down a rifle barrel."

"That's mighty tall talk, coming from a coward who uses a hideout gun. A *man* wears his weapons openly."

Fargo walked slowly to the exit.

"The first man I see step through this door behind me," he said as he backed out of the cantina, "is going to glory."

Keeping one eye on the open doorway, the other on the dark street, Fargo headed slowly toward the livery, sticking to the shadows.

The sudden racket of panicked horses nickering froze him in midstep. Just then he whiffed the acrid stench of smoke—and a moment later, saw huge tongues of orange flame licking upward from the hayloft of the livery.

Even as Fargo broke into a mad dash, he heard a female scream in horrifying pain and agony that could only mean death. It came from the little shack next to the livery, already totally engulfed in flames.

Fargo tried to approach it, but was driven back by heat so intense it singed his eyebrows. Anyone still inside was past help, but the livery wasn't yet totally ablaze. As shouts of "Fire!" and *"Fuego!"* broke out, Fargo burst through the double doors, hacking in the thick smoke.

Hooky McGhee lay dead near the first stall, his throat slashed from ear to ear. Fargo threw open the stall gates, freeing the trapped horses. The moment he burst back outside into the clear, leading his Ovaro, a voice rang out. *"There!* There's the son of a bitch that started the fire!"

Fortunately for Fargo, Hooky hadn't yet stripped the Ovaro of tack before he was killed. Fargo swung into leather, wheeled his horse, and smacked the pinto's rump hard even as a hail of hot lead hummed and whizzed past his ears.

2

Skye Fargo quirted the reins across the Ovaro's withers, quickly getting beyond effective bullet range.

He could hear the rapid drumbeat of mounted pursuers, and Fargo tossed some harmless lead over his shoulder just to keep them honest. Even bad shots could hit a horse if they got close enough. Dropping a man's mount from under him was common practice around here. Old Mexico's infamous *ley fuga,* or "flight law," still encouraged such acts on the blanket assumption that flight was always evidence of guilt.

But the offended citizens turned vigilantes were no serious threat, for the moment. Not when the Ovaro was in the mix. The stallion had not been grained for several days, but graze had been plentiful. And Fargo rarely pushed his horse beyond a fast trot, preferring to save the animal's bottom for a hard run—such as now. Neither the vigilantes' horses nor their trail skills could match Fargo's.

Nevertheless, he knew the fat was in the fire now. This mistaken-identity mess could get ugly in a hurry. On the frontier, horse thieves, card crimpers, killers of women or children, and arsonists were shot like barnyard rats. And (judging from that bloodcurdling scream he'd heard) Fargo was now presumed rapist, arsonist *and* woman-killer.

He reached a fork in the trail and took the right fork, bearing east. This fork was the dustiest, and he wanted to leave an obvious trail. A few hundred yards later, he drew rein and vaulted out of the saddle, leading the Ovaro into a piñon thicket beside, and slightly above, the trail.

Fargo tied the bridle reins to some weak branches, so the Ovaro wouldn't snap the reins if they had to pull foot in a hurry. Then he thumbed reloads into his Colt and filled the empty loops on his cartridge belt from a fresh box of ammo.

He had to be ready in case his ruse was discovered. This was a well-hidden position. Between his sixteen-shot Henry and the six beans in the wheel of his Colt, he could make it plenty lively for the exposed townies, should they rush his position.

The vigilantes Fargo could avoid, for that hotheaded crowd of tumbleweed tinhorns had little discipline or skill. But the nearest law, as best Fargo could recall, was the sheriff in Springer, twenty-five miles southwest of here.

His name was Sam Rafferty. Assuming he was still alive and packing a star, he was a good man to let alone. There was also a competent U.S. marshal, with deputies, in Santa Fe, and bored soldiers at Fort Union more than eager to hunt down raping, woman-killing arsonists.

The rataplan of approaching hooves scattered Fargo's thoughts. He left his Colt leathered, and levered a round into the breech of the Henry. He could see the trail clearly in the silver-white moonlight.

Five riders flashed past, among them the man who had tried to pull a fox play in the cantina. Fargo waited to see if they'd take the bait or double back.

They apparently took the bait. Fargo waited five minutes or so. When no one returned, he booted his Henry. Before he swung into leather again, he carefully checked his bit, bridle, girth, latigos, and stirrups.

Then he followed his own back-trail to the fork in the trail and took the left fork this time.

Fargo's plan was to find a safe spot and make a cold camp for a few hours. Then he could sneak back into Chico Springs and search for signs left by whoever murdered the hostler, then torched the shack and the livery. Every man left a trail, and Skye Fargo meant to dog this one even if it led straight into hell.

"Pile on the agony," he muttered when he spotted lights burning ahead, alongside the trail. Was another chase coming up, complete with whistling lead?

A few cautious minutes later, however, and he was gaping in pure astonishment.

At a carriage. *A real, by-God carriage,* Fargo marveled. One that might have been plucked right out of Hyde Park. Fancy green japanned wood varnished to a shine, quilted-satin seats, two gold-plated running lamps, even a liveried driver.

"Timely met, my good man! Timely met! Might I implore your assistance? I am escorting two ladies and appeal to your chivalry."

The lamps provided good lighting. The speaker was dressed in a swallowtail and a topper. A strong and vigorous man in his forties, his genteel manners and fancy tailoring were at odds with his raw-knuckled hands, and eyes like cold black chips of obsidian.

Fargo wasn't bothered, however, by the flap holster visible under the man's open coat. It was worn in plain view. Besides, anyone traveling these parts unarmed was either a Quaker or a fool.

A female voice suddenly spoke from inside the carriage.

"Correction, Nathan. That's *one* lady and a so-called lady's maid."

The speaker was a coldly attractive woman a few years younger than the man. The carriage door stood open, and Fargo saw she held a fancy satin reticule in the lap of her emerald ball gown. She lifted her hem and stepped down, assisted by the man she called Nathan.

"Of course, my dear, of course," the man muttered, turning his attention immediately back to Fargo. "We've broken down, sir. Appears to be the rear axle."

"Broken down, my sweet aunt," tossed in a second male voice.

It belonged to a younger, leaner, cockier version of Nathan. He had just stepped out from the shadows beyond the light.

"That brainless old Sancho up there," he added, meaning the elderly Mexican driver, "is blind as a cave bat. Ran plumb over a boulder and snapped an axle."

Fargo swung down, throwing the reins forward so the Ovaro would stand in place. Fargo dropped on all fours, peering under the slanting carriage. The "boulder" in question was hardly even a large rock. And the axle had broken, but not snapped in two. The difference was crucial.

He stood up, slapping the dust off his hands. "I wouldn't fault your driver, folks. No offense, this is a mighty handsome conveyance. But it's not built for these rocky, washboard roads."

The lippy kid didn't seem to like this remark. He moved a few steps closer, sizing up Fargo. The punk was toting a big-bore Remington in a canvas holster tied down low. His cavalry boots were shined to a high gloss, and he wore a low-crowned black hat with a rattlesnake-skin band.

" 'No offense'?" the kid repeated, his voice sharp with challenge. "Well, *I'm* offended. Since when does drifter trash like you tell your betters what to drive?"

"Since he's right, Butch," the older man interceded smoothly—so smooth, Fargo thought, that he was oily—"maybe you should just simmer down and butt out."

"Why, hell, Pa, he—"

"I said butt out," the father repeated, a sudden knife edge to his tone.

He faced Fargo again, all smiles. "Please forgive my son's bad manners, sir. Butch is at that stage in life where he perceives insults to his budding manhood everywhere. My name, by the way, is Nathan Robinson. I prefer Nate."

He extended his hand courteously, and Fargo gave him a grip. Fargo loathed the idea of using "summer names," especially when he was shaking a man's hand. But Antonio Two Moons had recognized him earlier. It would be dicey to noise his real name about.

"Pleased to meetcha. I'm Pete Helzer," he told Robinson.

"My wife, Cynthia, Mr. Helzer," Robinson said, nodding toward the frowning woman in the emerald gown. Fargo saw her tipple from a flask. "And her maid, Roberta."

Fargo had been wondering where the second woman was. She stepped down from the carriage now. Both Nathan Robinson and his son hastened to assist her. Fargo took one look at her and realized why the wife had no love for her maid.

Roberta wore a simple, robin's-egg blue dress cinched fetchingly tight at her hourglass waist. Lustrous blond hair was pulled back under a silver comb. Fargo took in those polished-apple cheeks and cornflower blue eyes, the heart-shaped lips just perfect for sweet, endless kissing.

He touched his hat.

"Ladies," he said, emphasizing the plural and earning a frown from Cynthia Robinson. Roberta's gaze, however, swept him from hat to heels—a long sweep.

"We live in Springer," Nate Robinson added. "We're returning from a social function in Raton. Could you possibly ride me into Chico Springs so that I might rent a conveyance at the livery there?"

That plan, Fargo realized, was as useless for them as it was suicidal for him. There *was* no livery in Chico Springs now. And when Fargo did return, it had better be secretly unless he was tired of breathing.

But neither was it his way to avoid helping stranded travelers, especially with females in their party.

"We could do that, Nate," Fargo replied. "But it's a lot of time and trouble, and there's five of you with your driver—given the size of Chico Springs, that almost surely means a buckboard."

"I *won't* be tossed about like cattle!" Cynthia Robinson protested before a sharp hiccup cut her off.

"I've got a suggestion," Fargo hastily intervened. "The axle isn't snapped clean through, only broken. We can prop it up level with stones, then thoroughbrace it with plenty of rawhide straps. It won't hold up long and it'll ride rough. But if you nurse it slow, you'll make it to Springer."

Fargo wasn't worried about the delay at his end. He needed to kill some time, anyway, before he returned to Chico Springs to look for the killer's trail. As for the citizens' posse, they were convinced Fargo had taken that right fork. They'd keep riding hell-for-leather until their mounts were lathered and spent.

"A thoroughbrace, eh?" Robinson repeated, rubbing his chin. "That might be just the ticket."

Fargo was already picking up flat rocks to use for leveling the broken axle. He saw Roberta watching him. She waited until Nate and his blowhard boy were locked in some private, heated dialogue. Then she slipped away to join Fargo.

"Pete?"

Fargo was late replying—he had rattled off the fake name so quickly he'd almost forgotten it. Besides, Roberta's sweetheart lips glistened with moisture in the far edge of the flattering lamplight. He whiffed the intoxicating aroma of her lilac cologne.

"Hmm?" he finally responded.

"My name is Roberta Jeanette Davis. But I go by Bobbie Jean with folks I like."

"You like me?"

Again that long sweep of her bewitching blue eyes.

"Right down to the ground," she assured him. "You really a drifter, like Butch called you?"

Fargo nodded. Butch had also called him "trash," and Fargo would remember that choice of words. All in good time, Butch Robinson would be called out on that direct insult.

"I'll never sink down roots," Fargo admitted. "Friend of mine calls it the tormentin' itch."

"Well, drifter . . . us girls get that itch, too. If you ever 'drift' into Springer, don't be shy. You can stick the toes of your boots under *this* gal's skirt any old time."

Fargo grinned. "You little vixen. You know I'm gonna have you on my mind now."

Her laughter was musical, teasing. "Good, that's the point. Make sure you picture me naked, too."

His grin widened. "That's already got started."

"The real me's even better, long-tall. Get to Springer, hear?"

Damn, thought Fargo. Bobbie Jean was starting the night's second fire—in his loins. This was woman-scarce country, and by now he had started to gaze longingly at knotholes in old outhouses.

But it didn't seem likely, at the moment, that they'd ever get the chance to put this new fire out. Not when, before long, half the hotheads in New Mexico Territory would likely be trying to put a load of blue whistlers into his belly.

"Hey, drifter!" Butch Robinson called out sharply to Fargo. "You aim to fix that axle or keep on bothering that woman?"

Cynthia Robinson, who struck Fargo as well into her cups, laughed sarcastically.

"Oh, she's 'bothered,' all right, Butchie boy," she taunted. "Like a queen in heat is bothered by a tom. Isn't it ironic? This unshaven frontiersman causes the same reaction in her that she causes in you and your father. And I don't blame her. This rustic fellow may not wear the latest fashions, but he strikes me as a *man*, not a monster behind a mask."

"Stow the chin-wag," Butch snarled at her. "You ain't even my real ma, you got no right—"

"Shut up, son," Nate Robinson cut in, his suave tone and manner suddenly brooking no defiance. "You'll respect your stepmother *and* Mr. Helzer. Stop calling him names and snapping orders at him. Roberta? Come over here, dear. Don't bother the man—he has work to do."

"I swear, I'll castrate both those filthy bastards," Fargo heard Bobbie Jean mutter as she obeyed Robinson.

During all this, the elderly Mexican driver had joined Fargo.

"My back is not so strong as yours, young man," he apologized. "But tell me what to do, and I will help."

Fargo dropped a stack of rocks near the back of the disabled carriage. The others were out of earshot.

"Ain't never met a Mexican nor Spanish fellow yet actually named Sancho," Fargo said. "Nor an Indian named John."

The two men shared a quiet laugh.

"I call myself Esteban," the silver-haired, aristocratic-looking driver replied. "Esteban Robles. But to *idiotas* like Butch Robinson, we who have lived here for centuries before his people are all Sanchos or greasers."

"That boy needs to have his attitude adjusted," Fargo agreed as he crawled under the carriage. "Esteban, you get ready with a rock. Each time I say 'heave,' slide one under the parts that are sagging. This ain't exactly a one-horse buggy—we'll take her up a jolt at a time."

Neither of the Robinson males even offered to help as Fargo, by sheer dint of will and muscle, got the axle almost back to its normal angle. Despite his age, Esteban was a nimble helper.

"Now we'll brace it good," Fargo explained, returning from his saddlebags with a supply of tough rawhide strips. "I'll need your help to hold 'em down tight while I wrap."

As they worked, Fargo remarked, "I've noticed how neither you nor Bobbie Jean are too fond of your employers?"

"Do not be fooled by their fine tailoring. Both of these men would steal dead flies from a blind spider."

Esteban sighed. "Once, Señor Helzer, I owned all the land between Las Cruces and El Paso del Norte. Now?" He shrugged. "A lickspittle for pompous fools with innocent blood on their hands. *Pero no doy por vencido.* But I don't give up."

This wasn't the time or place to ask about that "innocent blood" reference. Esteban's remark also confirmed Fargo's suspicion, based on the man's age and bearing, that he was one of the displaced Spanish grandees—noblemen who had been granted huge tracts of Southwest land by the king of Spain. Land abruptly stripped from them when the United States won the Mexican War.

"That should do it," Fargo announced, sliding back out and dusting himself off.

" 'Bout damn time," Butch complained. "You—*unh*!"

Butch fell silent when Fargo slapped him so hard the kid staggered backward. Fargo's left hand snaked out, grabbed the big-bore Remington, and flung it off into the brush. His next slap put the kid on the ground.

Butch came up cursing, and Fargo's heel smashed him full in the face. This time he stayed down, groaning like a hungover drunk.

All this took mere seconds. Fargo saw Nate Robinson reach inside his coat, but the Trailsman had already shucked out his Colt.

16

"Ease off, Nate," he advised mildly. "I've got no dicker with you. But that yapping pup you call a son had best learn some manners. He ever insults me again to my face, he won't get off with an ass-whipping."

Nate Robinson removed the handkerchief from his pocket and swiped at his brow.

"Pete, I take your point. He is indeed a yapping, ungrateful pup, and you haven't offended *me*. I was only going for my gun in case you tried to shoot him."

"Fair enough. I'd do the same for my own kin."

"But I'm afraid you just bought yourself six feet of real estate," Nate added. "Butch is indeed mouthy and immature. But he's also entered more than one hundred shooting contests and won every one of them. He spends three hours a day practicing his draw. And he holds a grudge until it grows mold. If I were you, Pete, I'd clear out of this territory."

"You're *dead,* you son of a bitch!" Butch snarled through a bubbling mouthful of blood. "You *hear* me? Lemme get my gun, you smug bastard, and we'll put paid to it right now!"

But Fargo already had enough on his plate as it was. He didn't have time for a pissing fight with this self-styled gunslick.

He stirruped and tossed a leg over the saddle bow.

"Sorry, junior," he told Butch. "Business to tend to. But we'll be huggin'."

Fargo cast one last, wistful glance at Bobbie Jean. She looked down toward her hemline, reminding him of her promise: *Any old time, long-tall.*

With a regretful sigh, Fargo clucked to his Ovaro, heading into the dark maw of the night.

Butch Robinson's taunts chased him like an enraged dog snapping at his heels.

"You're a goddamn coward, Helzer, hear me? A spineless, milk-livered coward! I'll *kill* you, you son of a bitch, you *hear* me?"

3

Riding silently and cautiously under a thin white wafer of moon, Fargo gradually made his way back to Chico Springs.

The night sky was cloudy and scant of stars, forcing him to rely on his ears as much as his eyes. The wind gusted sharply at times, shrieking through the hills and ravines. More often it made the steady, mournful sound some attributed to La Llorona, the sad and ghostly Weeping Woman doomed to eternally wander New Mexico mourning for her baby, slaughtered by the conquistadors.

A coyote howled from a ridge or two over. Its long, ululating cry ended in a series of yipping barks. The lonely sound, in that windswept vastness, made the hair on Fargo's nape stiffen.

He couldn't put it to words, but something unique and haunting about this storied region always drew him back, danger be damned. It affected many men that way, even transforming some into madmen who tried to turn moonbeams into gold. Like Gran Quivira, the city of gold that Coronado chased like a shadow across a fool's dream.

But tonight, Fargo knew, he was chasing no myths, no shadows, no fools. Just a cold-blooded killer with a taste for dispensing hellfire.

Of course Fargo was also out to save his own hide. Now that the telegraph had reached the Southwest, it wouldn't be long at all before wanted posters were plastered to walls between El Paso and Durango. Posters carrying his name and description.

Saving his own skin, however, had become a reflex for Skye Fargo. He had more powerful motivations for returning to Chico Springs.

Hooky McGhee had been cut down brutally. And that poor, doomed woman . . . though Fargo had never met her, her agonized scream as she burned to death had been seared into his memory for life.

In a sense, they had both been killed on Fargo's watch. That made it personal.

He would not, could not rest easy until a sick, murdering, scum-sucking cockroach on two legs answered for this. Nor was it only vengeance—this killer had to be stopped before more innocents were incinerated in their sleep.

Fargo, violating one of his own survival rules, was lost in gloomy reverie when the Ovaro suddenly tensed under him and shied to the left side of the trail.

Fargo's thoughts scattered like startled birds, and pure reflex kicked in. He spotted motion from the corner of his right eye even as he filled his hand, slewing around in the saddle to fire.

"Katy Christ," he said aloud in disgust directed at himself. "The ever-vigilant Trailsman."

He had very nearly plugged a tumbleweed, rolling and bouncing on a sudden wind gust. They sometimes blew in this far from the desolate plains to the east.

The incident reminded Fargo to focus his senses as he approached the wooded hills overlooking Chico Springs. Even so, he spared some attention to the matter of Nate Robinson and his trick-shooter whelp, Butch.

Unlike the vigilantes chasing him, Fargo usually tried not to stack his conclusions higher than his evidence. But neither did he ignore a gut hunch. And this latest hunch told him he'd be meeting Nate and Butch again—not just to settle a personal grudge, either.

Fargo had ridden as close to town as he dared. He'd learned from hard experience that even lazy dogs tended to bark at night when they whiffed an unfamiliar horse.

He stepped out of leather and ground-hitched the Ovaro in good graze shielded by pines. He approached the western end of town on foot, gliding among shadows, covering his advance with wind noise. Fortunately, a house blocked him from the view of the sentry leaning against the stack of lumber.

Fargo had waited for hours before returning. So he already knew the "regulators" had returned, their horses blowing lather. As Fargo had predicted, their enthusiasm had waned as they neared their soft beds. These were townies, not Texas Rangers.

Nonetheless, he spotted a lone figure hovering near the still-smoking ruins of the shack and the livery.

Fargo loosened his Arkansas Toothpick in its boot sheath. Then he drew his Colt and thumbed back the hammer. Sticking to an apron of shadows, he stole a few steps closer, listening.

He heard what sounded like a peon saying his beads in Spanish. And he did indeed spot the rope sandals of a peasant, though not one wearing the usual *manta*. Instead, this one wore his church suit.

Realizing who it was, Fargo seated the hammer and holstered his Colt.

"Don't be scared, Antonio," he called out in a whisper. "I'm coming closer. *Con permiso?*"

"*Sí*, Señor Fargo, please do join me. I hate solitude when I am sad. And I am the only man left in Chico Springs who knows you are not a murderer."

Even in the dim light, Fargo could see tears streaking Antonio Two Moons' round face. The cantina owner was staring toward a spot in the smoldering ashes.

"I loved Elena," he confessed, as if ashamed by his presumption for loving her. "For years. It was foolish, *cómo no*. I am a poor *indio*, forbidden by law from even riding a horse or owning a gun. Never could I hope to marry her. But it did not matter to me. To me? She was the fairest flower of them all. Just the chance to see her, speak with her—these things were the breath in my nostrils, Señor Fargo."

"So Elena was her name?"

"Yes. Elena Vargas y Diego. A fine girl, *señor*. Through all she suffered, her faith was never shaken. 'Never plow on Sunday, Antonio,' she would tell me when I had my bean fields. 'Or you will plow for the devil in all eternity.' "

At first Fargo was confused. Antonio was staring

fixedly at one spot. Fargo looked closer and noticed a lumpy white powder.

Then, realizing what it was, anger tightened his throat. Quicklime. Poured over the unspeakable remains to hold down the smell and dissolve them faster.

Antonio saw the realization in Fargo's troubled face.

"It is true," the Pueblo Indian said. "She will never rest in peace at the *camposanto*. How long must her soul now hover in torment, *ay Dios*! So badly burned, the remains were beyond burying. She will dissolve into *polvo*, dust."

As Fargo glanced around, he reminded himself he still had no proof this fire was deliberate. But Hooky McGhee sure as hell didn't slice open his own throat, so the clues pointed to arson.

"Be right back," he told Antonio.

Fargo ducked into the alley between the two ruined structures. It was quick work to sort out one recent pattern of boot tracks and follow them up the sandy slope south of town.

He found a thicket where a man and a horse had obviously passed some time, perhaps a day or more. Tobacco juice stained the ground, and he'd made no effort to hide the crusts of some ash-pone he'd either dropped or discarded while eating. Fargo also spotted a pile of horse droppings and broke it open with the toe of his boot.

Almost dry inside, but not quite. In this summer heat, it couldn't be that old. And a fresh trail headed southwest—toward Springer.

Fargo, hunched to lower his profile, returned to Antonio.

"I didn't set that fire," he told him. "But it was deliberate, all right."

Antonio nodded. "*Sí*. And you saw how quickly it spread. This monster, he is a master of his sick craft, *verdad*?"

Damn straight, Fargo thought. Any murderer was a low and vile creature, and a woman- or child-killer the lowest of the low. But to kill *this* way . . .

Fargo glanced again at the quicklime and felt his will clench like a fist. The U.S. Army was definitely going to have to wait—even though his failure to show up soon would make him look even more guilty. Despite being light in the pockets, Fargo had a job to do first.

Antonio seemed to shake himself awake.

"Señor Fargo, *por Dios*! What are you doing here? The fools have already convicted you."

"Just needed to confirm a few things before I shove on."

"I tried to tell them about you. As they composed the *telegrama* to Santa Fe. I said to them, 'But it was only a few minutes, after the *gringo famoso* left the cantina, that we heard the first cries.' I said to them, *'El fuego* was too big, too hot already.' It must have been burning *before* you left."

Fargo grinned. "Let me guess—the mere facts didn't matter a jackstraw to them?"

"As you say, though I do not know this Jack Straw. And now, *señor,* you are subject to *ley fuga.*"

"Yeah," Fargo admitted. "Flight law. I had that on my mind earlier, when they were trying to blast me out from under my hat."

"You are now a fugitive," Antonio said with the sad fatalism this land bred in men. "You will not be hunted down to be arrested, but to be executed on sight. The posse and the hangman are one."

"I've faced rope justice before," Fargo assured him.

The two men shook hands. But as Fargo turned to leave, an earlier thought returned to him.

"Antonio?"

"Sí?"

"What do you hear about Nate Robinson and his son, from over in Springer?"

"Virgen de Guadalupe!"

Antonio hastily made the sign of the cross. Then he surprised Fargo by grabbing his arm and tugging him back farther from the smoking ruins.

"Sainted backsides! I beg you, do not utter that evil name so near where Elena's soul hovers in torment."

"Sorry," Fargo told him. "But I know nothing about them, that's why I had to ask. Why is the name evil?"

Antonio moved back even farther, lowering his voice.

"There are only *rumores,* stories one hears. You know about the scalp bounties in Chihuahua?"

Fargo nodded. "Started in 1840. Supposedly on Apache scalps."

"As you say—supposedly. But in truth, many people in Old and New Mexico have coarse black hair. It is said that Nate Robinson fought, down in Old Mexico, in the great war between *gringos* and the *Mexicanos.* That he stayed there after it was over, leading his own private army of scalpers. Apaches, Mexicans, Pueblos, Yaquis, it did not matter. His butchers killed any man, woman, or child with black hair. And with this blood money he now hopes to one day rule New Mexico as his own kingdom."

Fargo said nothing, only listening. Rumors about rich men, and their supposedly wicked pasts, abounded among the envious poor.

And yet . . . the story made sense, too. Many men had discovered, after mustering out from that bloody conflict in Mexico, that they had developed a taste for killing. The elitist and corrupt governor of Chihuahua was more than happy to "control the peasant problem" by paying foreign mercenaries to kill them.

"All right," Fargo said. "We'll call that a rumor, for now. What do you know about him for sure?"

"For sure? Not so much," Antonio admitted. "Only what I hear in my cantina. He is in the brick business. This I know for certain. Not adobe bricks. The kind made from red clay. Recently he built the territory's first furnace for baking them."

"Bricks?" Fargo repeated. "That's a tough sell down here, ain't it?"

"With the prices for lumber so high now, who knows? This Robinson, I hear, is the man to succeed at anything he tries. As they say, he likes to keep both hands on the reins. *De todo*—of everything."

"Including his wife's pretty maid?" Fargo prompted.

"*Claro.* Many men speak of her in my presence. I hear he and the son both compete for her . . . favors. And for this the wife calls her a whore. True, the girl does have an eye for the *hombres,* eh? But she despises Nate and Butch and will leave as soon as her brother can purchase her back."

"Purchase?" Fargo repeated, brows knitting in a puzzled frown. "Slavery ain't legal in the Territories."

"No. But she and the old man, Robles, are . . . *cómo se dice?*" Antonio tapped his teeth as a hint. "*Dientes,* teeth."

Fargo laughed. "You mean indentured servants?"

"*Eso,* the very thing. Such arrangements are legal in this area. Señor Fargo?"

"Yeah?"

"I understand what you are doing, and I wish you godspeed. You see, Elena, too, lost her family to scalpers. Murdered in front of her down in Sonora. But she was spared for her beauty, only to be repeatedly raped by her captors. She escaped and came north to Chico Springs. Only . . . to die like this."

Antonio looked away for a moment, swiping at his eyes. "*Que lastima!* It breaks my heart, the wrong of it. It is a wrong too great to be told. Please forgive my tears—I am not strong like you. I loved her so. Oh, how can such things be?"

Fargo hated to do it, but he had to leave Antonio alone with his grief. He squeezed the man's shoulder.

"Far as those tears, ain't nothing to be ashamed of, Antonio, in loving somebody. You just remember, this thing's a long way from over."

As he returned to the Ovaro, intending to pick up the killer's trail just outside of town, Fargo mulled Antonio's words.

He was right, Fargo was indeed strong. But was he strong enough to right wrongs "too great to be told"?

There was that scream in the night—a good woman's anguished cry of horrific agony—that would haunt Fargo to his grave. That scream would never disappear, nor would Elena Vargas y Diego get her life back. Neither would Hooky McGhee, and Antonio was the deep-feeling type who would carry this grief for life. Fargo himself knew what that was like, and he wouldn't wish it on an enemy.

Terrible damage was already done. But if Fargo dealt

justice to this killer, and as soon as possible, how many more screams would never have to be uttered?

"Well, I'll be a broomtailed son of a bitch," Butch Robinson muttered. "That musta been about the same time we—"

Nate Robinson held a hand out to silence his boy. The first broadsheets from that day's edition of the *Springer Clarion* had just been plastered up in the streets. Nate continued reading.

" 'The killer and arsonist is described as a tall, bearded man wearing buckskins and riding a pinto stallion. He has been identified as Skye Fargo, known widely as the Trailsman.' "

"Christ!"

Butch, whose lips looked swollen and bruised in the early morning sunshine, grabbed his old man's arm.

"Tall, bearded, buck—Pa, that was the jasper that fixed our axle last night! *Ho*-ly Hannah! I knew I shoulda put an air shaft through him."

"Hush it, you young fool," Nate snapped, finishing the story. " 'Fargo has scouted widely for the Army in the New Mexico Territory and is said to know the area well. He was last seen in Chico Springs, and a wide manhunt is already under way.' "

Nate chuckled, shaking his head at the vagaries of life. And the way Lady Luck could suddenly choose to smile on a man.

"You *believe* that ballsy son of a bitch?" Butch said. "Burns down half of Chico Springs, kills two people, then tells *me* he won't abide an insult. That bastard would stand in a breadline and demand toast."

The two men stood on the raw-plank boardwalk in front of Springer's only respectable hotel, the Dorsey. It had taken more than five hours for their disabled carriage to limp home last night, and both men were bleary-eyed with sleeplessness.

But this unexpected news perked up Nate like a tonic.

"Butch," he said, chuckling again, "at least *pretend* you've got more brains than a titmouse. Fargo didn't murder anybody or set any fire."

25

"Then why does it say right here—"

"Boy, learn to read character, not printer's ink. If Fargo was this kind of killer, you really think you'd still be alive today? He'd have snuffed your wick last night instead of just messing up your face."

"He mighta goddamn *tried*," Butch growled. But a moment later, confusion replaced his tough scowl. "I don't get it. Says here it was Fargo; you say it wasn't. What the hell?"

Nate ignored his son for a few moments, touching his hat politely as a woman in widow's weeds passed them. Then he gazed with proprietary pride over the town he had chosen as the seat of his soon-to-be financial empire.

Springer was a predominately Anglo community that had sprung up with the influx of whites into northern New Mexico, after the area became a U.S. Territory. Very little in Springer reflected the adobe-and-tile Spanish frontier style prevalent throughout the Southwest. And that's exactly why Nate had chosen it.

"Who was it?" Nate repeated. "Think about it a minute."

Nate waited for realization to dawn in his son's dull eyes. But it was like waiting for rain in the desert. When it came to shooting, Butch was the top hand, all right. But he wasn't the brightest spark in the campfire.

Nate sighed and gave his boy a clue. He nodded toward the freighting dock at the far end of town. Stacks of milled lumber awaited shipment to nearby communities such as Raton and Cimarron. Like Springer itself, those towns were experiencing a building boom and demanding lumber.

Butch stared at his father. "You don't mean . . . ?"

A slow smile divided Nate's face. He wore long, hanging sideburns of the type called Icadilly Weepers.

"Who else?" he replied. "You know the man's reputation. And according to his last wire, he's due to arrive about now, so we can settle on the price for his services."

Butch loosed a whistle. "See there? I warned you. They say that crazy bastard is six sorts of hell when he's on a tear. And looks like he's on one, all right."

"Yes," Nate agreed, putting a little more tooth enamel into his smile. "He is, isn't he?"

"And you *like* it?"

"Matter fact, chucklehead, I do. And so would you if you had the sense God gave a pissant."

Butch shook his head. "Old man, have you been grazing loco weed? It's one thing to torch some lumber. But your man is burning up women in their beds! We get linked to that, our hash is cooked."

Burning women in their beds? Nate knew that was small potatoes compared to the way he'd made his "seed money" as he called it. It wasn't his problem if the governor of Chihuahua made no distinctions between those with black hair—to Nate, those scalps were just cash money, pure and simple.

"*My* man?" Nate protested. "I beg to differ. It's 'Pete Helzer' they're after, sonny boy. Don't you see the beauty of it? Fargo knows he's in deep shit, or he wouldn't've made up that name last night. Now Weston can operate with a free hand while all eyes focus on Fargo."

"Sure," Butch said, catching on. "It works right in our favor, don't it?"

"Of course. If it's *just* stacks of lumber getting torched in this region, that notches the sights right on us. After all, who has a bigger stake in seeing lumber destroyed?"

Again Nate gazed around town. Unlike old native pueblos like Taos or Chimayo, Springer was definitely a lumber town—big, boxy, two-story frame buildings, many with high false fronts. And Nate Robinson meant to change all that, here and anywhere else in the territory where structures were going up.

Nate was convinced a man could make a fortune, here in the tree-rich but lumber-scarce West, in the brick-making business. Sawmills were still few and far between, and always remote from shipping points. Bricks, in contrast, could be baked right in transportation hubs like Springer, saving much time and expense.

It had cost him nearly every penny he had to build the area's first brick furnace. And orders were coming in slower than he'd expected. Folks were reluctant to build with brick because it required more time and labor than slapping up a frame structure. Many were still willing to pay outrageous prices for lumber.

But that thinking can be changed, Nate told himself. Again his eyes cut to the stacks of new boards. Let there suddenly be a critical shortage of lumber, and folks would *have* to buy bricks.

Butch's voice cut into his thoughts.

"Say, Pa . . . won't Sam Rafferty be getting up a posse to look for Fargo?"

"Eventually. But he's in Santa Fe, remember? Testifying in that case of the fellow accused of killing a federal paymaster."

Butch nodded. "Hell, that's right. And seeing how Rafferty's got no deputy, it'll fall to the Vigilance Committee."

"Which includes you, their crack shootist."

Butch stroked the walnut grips of his Remington. "I promised that lanky cockchafer last night I'd do for him. Next time he crosses my trail, he'll be taking a dirt nap."

"Judging from what I saw of Fargo last night, you won't likely see him until he wants to be seen. But do make a big show out of looking for him. Talk it up big. However, if you do actually see him, you'll do no such damn fool thing as kill him."

The rest of Butch's face turned almost as purple as his bruised mouth. Nate raised a hand to stifle the protest.

"Look, son, I don't care if you shoot him to wolf bait—eventually. But right now, for us, Fargo is the key to the mint. So long as he's taking the blame for arson fires around here, we need him alive and running free."

But by now Butch was losing interest in the conversation. Nate saw him gaze longingly down the street, in the direction of the Queen of Sheba. The saloon was a rambling frame structure located in an alley off the main street to placate the local bluenoses. It was owned by Moonshine Jones, who also oversaw a gaggle of whores working out of the rooms on the second floor. But Butch wasn't thinking about the whores.

"Think with your brain, not your cod," his father snapped at him. "If you had kept your hands off Bobbie Jean at home, your stepmother wouldn't have forced her to room in a whorehouse."

"Keep *my* hands off her? You're the one Cynthia's jealous of, not me. That's what I don't understand. You already get it regular, I don't. Plus Bobbie's more my age than yours. Why should you care if I get a little of that stuff now and then?"

"That's what the whores at the Queen of Sheba are for. Two dollars a whack, and no puling babies to keep you awake nights."

But Nate spoke absently. He was busy watching a young man exit the Dorsey and head down the street toward the freighting office and the stacks of milled lumber.

"Speaking of Bobbie Jean," he remarked, "there goes Jim Davis now to ship the day's orders."

"Yeah," Butch said glumly. "And once he sells that big order going down to Albuquerque, he'll have the money to pay off Bobbie Jean's contract. Won't neither of us get none then."

"You know my golden rule," his father replied confidently. "He who has the gold rules. Weston should be contacting me any time now, maybe even today. That lumber may never get shipped."

Nate tapped the broadside with the gold head of his walking stick. "Good chance this murdering arsonist, Skye Fargo, will strike first."

4

Skye Fargo rode all night, following the trail of an anonymous killer who was as pitiless and monstrous as any he'd ever hunted down.

The cutthroat and arsonist had taken no pains to cover the clues as to where he'd hidden in Chico Springs, nor to cover his trail as he first rode out. But Fargo quickly realized he was up against a trail-savvy foe.

Time and again he left clever false trails, forcing Fargo to waste time backtracking. And Fargo very nearly lost him altogether at the Canadian river, where the killer had waded upstream, left a false trail, then waded back downstream before again bearing southwest. All these moves were much quicker and easier for the killer to make than for Fargo to figure out from scant sign.

He's mighty damn careful, Fargo realized. And good at dodging pursuers. That only made him more dangerous.

The trail sneaked its way toward Springer, a fact that made Fargo nervous for several reasons—including Sheriff Sam Rafferty. Never mind that the lawman was getting a bit long in the tooth. Though his once eagle eyes were now bespectacled for reading, his aim was still true and his mind still sharp as a steel trap.

Then again, Fargo recalled, the lovely Bobbie Jean Davis had breathlessly urged him to visit her in Springer: *Girls get that tormentin' itch, too.* Fargo pictured her moist lips and double-handful waist, the blond hair like spun-gold sunshine. A light blonde like her usually had a silky, wispy bush below. . . .

Forced by such pleasant thoughts to adjust himself in

the saddle, Fargo reluctantly pushed the saucy beauty from his mind. And just in time: He was on the feather edge of riding smack into view of an Indian raiding party.

Fargo drew rein and swung down, quickly patting the Ovaro's neck to calm him before leading the stallion into a stand of piñons. He counted six riders in single file, backlit by the moon and topping a rise just ahead of him. They rode small, fourteen-hand mustangs with hair bridles and sheepskin pads for saddles.

Even before he could clearly make out their hide leggings, knee-length moccasins, and loincloths, he guessed they must be Apaches—one of the few tribes Fargo knew of that weren't superstitious about leaving their campfires after dark. The dozens of peaceful local tribes, Pueblos like Antonio Two Moons, were mostly Christianized farmers and herders now. They minded their own business and had given outsiders little trouble since the Pueblo Revolt of 1680.

But that left four dangerous tribes—Apaches, Comanches, Navajos, and Utes—raiding in this area. That included much slave-taking of women and children, and Fargo had been in the thick of that mare's nest before. This bunch wasn't painted for war, but with Apaches he could never be certain. Unlike a Sioux or Cheyenne, they might kill a man on the spur of the moment, without any religious rituals first.

Or they might nod politely and pass by. Fargo would rather not roll the dice if he could avoid the gamble altogether.

They were passing by only about fifteen feet in front of him now. He had made sure to duck downwind so their mustangs wouldn't whiff the Ovaro. He recognized the clan notchings of both Jicarillas and Mescaleros, Apache groups once native to northern New Mexico, where they often still raided the mountain villages.

This bunch had evidently also raided military outposts in Old Mexico—they carried sturdy Mexican Army carbines and wore crossed bandoleers bristling with ammunition.

Fargo already had enough on his plate with vigilantes and the law out for his hide. Now he was also going to have to dodge some of the toughest and most fearless warriors in the entire red nation. A familiar churning of his guts told him their paths would cross again— especially now that he, too, had become a hunted creature of the night.

"We jumped over a snake that time, boy," Fargo muttered as he swung up onto the hurricane deck again.

Fortunately, the slow pace of tracking had been easy on the Ovaro. But by sunrise Fargo had been awake for twenty-four hours, much of it spent climbing on and off his horse, squatting over faint signs, hanging halfway out of the saddle to watch the ground. He was worn out, and knew he should have spread his blankets for a few hours. But he had cut fresh sign on his quarry, in the grassland and hill country about ten miles northeast of Springer.

Trouble was, he was now caught in the open, and dawn didn't linger in the vast emptiness of the Southwest. Already he was casting a shadow.

Fargo paused to study the surrounding terrain. His weathered eyes narrowed to slits in the already glaring sunlight.

The trained vision of a veteran scout took everything in at once. Fargo deliberately avoided focusing on anything specific. He simply let the entire landscape flow up to his eyes, as he had once explained the elusive art of scouting to a young cavalry officer.

That's how he spotted the flash of what he guessed were binoculars, and then the riders—still only flyspecks on the horizon—bearing down on his position at a full gallop.

"Ah, hell," he said with quiet resignation. "Well, old warhorse, we're up against it again. Gets old, don't it?"

Word was out about Skye Fargo, woman-killer.

He thumped the Ovaro's ribs with his heels, and the stallion was off like a scalded dog. This latest escape would mean losing the trail Fargo was working. But by now he was convinced his man was headed, for whatever hellish purpose, straight toward Springer.

Fargo had a good lead. But he was also trapped in wide-open country with miles to go before he reached the pine ridges and brushy hollows north of Springer. It wasn't too long before a couple of sharpshooters opened up behind him with long-range repeating rifles.

Fargo watched divots of grass flying every which way as bullets chunked and thumped all around him, arriving well before the sound of the rifle reports. Just ahead he spotted the far-flung mounds of a prairie-dog town and rode right into the thick of them.

The bullet-savvy Ovaro hardly slowed, knowing this was a race for survival. But Fargo knew most horses tended to rattle, to shy away from places where expanses of green grass were dug up. He had once watched mustangers pen a bunch of wild horses simply by plowing a line around them during the night.

His ruse worked, and Fargo made it to cover, shaking his pursuers. But as he regretfully ran his fingers through his beard, he realized he was worm fodder if he didn't make some changes in his appearance—and damn quick.

There was an out-of-the-way trading post, on the south bank of Old Spanish Creek, run by a former Taos Trapper named Elkhorn John. Fargo hoped that word of his new fugitive status hadn't yet reached the old recluse.

"How they hangin', Elkhorn?" Fargo greeted him from the open doorway.

"One hangs lower'n the other," he complained. "Been gettin' any?"

"I'm holding my own," Fargo quipped, and both men laughed as they always did. It was their standard greeting ritual.

"What's the word these days?" Fargo added. "Ain't seen a newspaper in weeks."

"The word?" The crusty old cob snorted. "The hell does *this* child care? Only interest I got in a buncha damn flatlanders is to lighten their wallets."

"All right, you old goat, lighten mine."

Fargo bought a razor, shaving soap and mug, and, gritting his teeth, a complete set of the new "reach-me-downs"—mass-produced, ready-to-wear clothing. One of the stupidest damn inventions Fargo ever heard of. Hell, was the day coming when people would actually pay good money for paper to wipe their asses, too?

"Good-bye, old friend," he muttered as he lathered up his beard. "It's only temporary."

Using a clear pool beside the creek as his mirror, he shaved, astonished at how naked and pale his face looked now. He peeled off his buckskins and stuffed them into a saddlebag.

Wincing in disgust at the foreign feel, he dressed in his store-bought dungarees and shirt of stiff broadcloth. Fargo wasn't used to buttons, except when undoing them on a woman's clothing, and his fingers fumbled with them now.

He felt like a pilgrim, but Fargo had to admit he looked vastly different without his beard and buckskins. His big problem now was the Ovaro.

True, pintos were among the most commonly seen horses on the frontier. But usually only free Indians rode stallions, most whites preferring to geld their male horses to control them around mares. Fargo could risk riding in open country, but dare not take the Ovaro into any larger towns.

He was tensed for action as he rode the final leg of the approach to Springer. But he passed no one on the road except a few farmers in straw hats, pushing a drove of mules. They hardly spared him a glance.

The Sangre de Cristo range filled the right horizon, sliced by gullies on the lower slopes. Things were humming around here since Fargo's last visit—he even passed a few spreads with small herds of cattle.

Mostly, though, just little nester farms. Sometimes the dwellings on these smaller homesteads were little more than brush shanties covered with wagon canvas. An intricate system of *acequias* irrigated the corn, beans, and squash, all controlled by a large "mother ditch" with huge gates.

Fargo watered the Ovaro good before stripping him to the neck leather and rubbing him down with an old feed sack. Then he left him on a long tether in a well-hidden copse about a quarter mile outside of town. He would bring oats back later and feed the stallion from his hat.

Lugging his saddle, with the Henry booted, Fargo hoofed it into town.

Springer, too, was booming since Fargo last passed through. Only six months earlier, the town had become a spur on the Topeka and Santa Fe line. There was a big new mercantile in the heart of town, a new harness shop, and—bad news for the Trailsman—a Western Union window on one side of the Overland Stage and Freight office.

And more stacks of lumber, he noticed. Just like in Chico Springs.

A few passersby studied him from caged eyes, making sweat bead up under Fargo's hatband. He would be forced to spend the last of his money on a room just to have a place to lay low. But first he headed for an alley off the main street.

The best place to get information in a hurry would be from the talkative and friendly owner of the Queen of Sheba. Fargo didn't remember his name, and hoped his own altered appearance was good enough to trick the owner's memory.

The Queen of Sheba's dual purpose was obvious the moment he slapped open the batwings and stepped into the dark, smoke-hazed interior. A gaudy faro layout was prominently positioned to draw in the suckers like flies to a molasses barrel. And instead of the usual calendars advertising O. F. Winchester's latest firearms, the flocked wall behind the bar sported a mural of fleshy nudes—most likely painted by some talented itinerant artist.

"Mornin', friend. You here to wet your pecker or your beak? Or both?"

The speaker was a rail-thin, pinch-faced man with a scruffy red beard and a goiter. He stopped wiping off the bar long enough to massage his jaw and wince.

"Got special-made choppers coming from St. Louis," he apologized. "Some mining-camp dentist made me these wooden teeth, but they hurt like the dickens. Jones is the name. Moonshine Jones. I took that front name after Lucas County, Ohio, voted to go dry and the Temperance League ran me out of town for operating a still. Free country, my freckled ass. Psalm-singing hypocrites."

"Name's Dave Tutt," Fargo lied, giving his second summer name in as many days.

He crossed a raw plank floor covered with sawdust.

No one was drinking at the bar, but a tall redhead in a low-cut velvet gown had drawn a circle of men and kept the faro rig's card counter clicking.

Moonshine slapped a bottle of who-shot-John and a jolt glass onto the counter.

"Loop your lips over that, Dave. Ain't bad whiskey if you put your fist through the wall to help it down."

Fargo grinned and tossed back a shot. The liquor was indeed cheap panther piss, but he welcomed the bracing feel as it burned in a straight line to his gut.

When Fargo fished in his pocket, Moonshine waved him off. "On the house. When a fellow comes into a saloon this early, carrying his saddle, he ain't celebrating a bonanza."

He winked and added: "The girls upstairs sometimes do charity work in the morning, if they like a man's look."

Fargo grinned. "I'll keep that in mind. I prefer volunteers over paid labor."

Moonshine poured him another jolt. "How 'bout a plate of eggs and *chorizo*? Warn you, though, it'll be a belly burner. My cook's a Mexer, and she puts chili peps in everything."

Fargo nodded gratefully. He'd had nothing to eat since the beans and tortillas yesterday in Chico Springs.

Moonshine called something in Spanish toward a kitchen behind the bar. Fargo glanced toward a doorless archway in the side wall. Heavy velvet curtains were tied back to reveal an attached parlor like a sultan's harem. He glimpsed a fancy, serpentine-backed sofa, overstuffed chairs, lamps with red-fringed shades, a big giltwood-framed mirror.

Moonshine set a plate in front of him. Fargo noticed a sawed-off cuestick dangling from the saloon owner's wrist.

"It's just for show," he told Fargo. "Hell, if I was any skinnier I'd need rocks in my pockets to walk in the wind."

He fell silent and studied Fargo's face.

"You know," Moonshine said, "I'm one to remember a man's eyes. Seems like, while back, fellow came in here, had lake blue eyes just like yours."

"Mighta been me," Fargo said around a mouthful of food. "I've been through Springer a few times, heading down to Santa Fe."

"Well . . . seems this fellow had a thick beard, wore buckskins."

Fargo kept chewing, letting the remark just lay there between them. The hell were his options but to follow this trail through? Moonshine held the reins, at the moment.

Outside, hoofs clopped on the hardpack of Main Street.

"Good grub," Fargo said, shoveling in another bite.

"The thing of it is," Moonshine added, "I can't help recalling this fellow. See, these three *vaqueros* 'invited' him to play stud poker. He agreed, but quite correctly called for a fresh deck. As I recall, his exact words were, 'These cards got more nicks in 'em than a cowtown lamppost.' "

It took an effort for Fargo not to grin. He'd said exactly those words, all right.

"Long story short," Moonshine resumed, "the *vaqueros* took offense. Words were exchanged, the bearded fellow questioned the virginity of someone's sister, a knife was flashed. Next thing I knew, there were three holes in the wall and three Mexican cowboys bleeding in the street, calling for their *mamacitas*."

"Wall looks fine now," Fargo remarked.

"That's the amazing thing, Dave. This fellow paid me twice what the damage cost and apologized for the bad manners of the *vaqueros*. Now . . . if you was to tell me that a man with mettle like that in him was a cold-blooded killer? Why, hell, I'd laugh in your face. No matter *what* a bunch of half-assed peckerwoods in Chico Springs swore. You catch my drift . . . Dave Tutt?"

Moonshine's red-rimmed, gimlet eyes bored into his.

Fargo nodded, deciding he could trust him. Moonshine knew all about being hounded and persecuted.

"Moonshine?"

The familiar female voice startled Fargo. He glanced into the mirror behind the bar and recognized Bobbie Jean Davis stepping out of the gaudy whorehouse parlor.

"Yeah, sugar babe?" Moonshine called to her.

Fargo pulled his hat lower and turned away from her line of sight. She looked pretty in a dark blue skirt and a frilly white shirtwaist. Today her blond hair fell unrestrained in back, the bold new fashion Europeans called "the American style."

"The Robinsons had a breakdown on the road, and I got in late last night," she said. "So I'm taking the day off until noon, whether Cynthia likes it or not, the snooty bitch. If Nate or Butch show up here, tell them the usual lie—I'm out. This time say I'm at my dressmaker's. They don't know her."

"Got it, hon."

Fargo watched her return to the parlor, hips rolling like a prospector's rocker box. She headed up a narrow staircase at the rear of the parlor.

"You're telling me," Fargo remarked, "that Cynthia Robinson's maid is one of your sporting gals, too?"

Moonshine snorted. "Christ, don't I wish? So you know her?"

"Not in the Old Testament sense."

"Yeah, get in line. Well, she's sitting on a gold mine, brother. I've told her that. A sweet little piece, ain't she?"

Fargo attacked the last of his breakfast. "Looks good, but you know what they say. It ain't the steak, it's the sizzle."

"Trust me, brother, she sizzles. But she doesn't work here, just boards. Robinson's snotty-assed wife threw her out of their house. And Bobbie Jean couldn't get a room at the Dorsey because Cynthia put out the lie that she was once a whore in Amarillo."

"Let me guess," Fargo said. "The wife tossed her because Nate and Butch are both in rut for Bobbie Jean?"

Moonshine smashed a fly with a corner of his bar rag, then nodded.

"Nate *or* Butch would pay her a sheik's ransom just to lick it once. But Bobbie Jean enjoys humping too much to ever turn it into a business and kill the fun. And she likes to choose her men. She doesn't pick one often, but when she does, mister, she leaves 'em limping for a week."

Moonshine hooked a thumb toward the ceiling. "Her

38

bed's right over the bar. When she gets into her stride? Afterward, there's an inch of plaster dust on the bar. Even my bargain-rate whores don't break as many bed boards in one night as Bobbie Jean can."

Fargo filed these tantalizing tidbits away.

"Got any rooms available?" he asked.

"Yeah, I'd ask, too. Nothing right now. But there's six gals upstairs and Fanny at the faro table. If a fellow makes friends, he can sometimes wangle a bed for a few nights."

Fargo hated to do it, but he'd have to check into the overpriced Dorsey for now. He couldn't just wander around, waiting to be recognized and shot.

"Sheriff Rafferty still around?" Fargo inquired as he slid off the stool and hefted his saddle.

"He's down in Santa Fe on court business." Moonshine paused, then added: "And the stubborn old mule won't hire a deputy—says he can't trust any man he knows. Which, until he gets back, leaves this town in the hands of our fair-minded, law-and-order Vigilance Committee."

Fargo caught the sarcastic warning. He nodded and headed outside, angling across the street toward the Dorsey. The morning was well advanced now and the street boiling with activity. Fargo felt like the bull's-eye on a target.

The splendor of the Dorsey's main lobby convinced him this featherbed palace would clean him out. Bronze-framed mirrors covered the walls, and two huge fireplaces were mantled with blood onyx, marble, and slate. A group of elegantly dressed young ladies shared a large circular sofa with a central headrest. They had obviously just detrained—one of them was complaining bitterly about cinder holes in her new silk taffeta gown.

"That will be five dollars, Mr. Tutt," a perfumed clerk wearing a stiff paper collar told him. "In advance," he added, casting a dubious glance at the half moons of dirt under Fargo's fingernails, then at his saddle and six-shooter.

Five dollars! Christ, thought Fargo, *that price should include a whore and a bottle.*

He was just fishing the last quarter-eagle gold piece

from his pocket when Butch Robinson, sided by several men carrying rifles, stepped into the lobby. The conversational buzz suddenly fell silent.

The moment Fargo saw how their eyes prowled the lobby, he realized they were part of the Vigilance Committee.

He snatched off his hat, just before Butch's eyes settled on him, and crammed it into a saddlebag. Fargo knew Butch had seen it last night. He took his key from the clerk and turned casually away from the front desk, heading toward the spiral staircase at the back of the lobby.

"Hey, you! Yeah, you carrying the saddle! Hold it right there, mister!"

As Fargo turned toward Butch's voice, he shifted the saddle to clear his drawing hand.

Butch stopped a few feet away, belligerent eyes measuring Fargo.

"What's your name, stranger?"

"What's that to you?"

Fargo didn't even see a blur. In less than an eyeblink, the big-bore Remington was aimed straight at his lights. *He must have* willed *it into his hand,* Fargo marveled.

"Let's try it one more time," Butch snarled.

"His name's Dave Tutt," the ashen-faced clerk volunteered.

"Tutt, huh?" Butch's hard little flint-chip eyes cut to the saddle. "What kind of horse you riding?"

"I *had* a chestnut gelding under this saddle. But two nights ago Apaches killed it and ate it. I was lucky to escape with my hair."

" 'Paches don't scalp, greenhorn. Anyhow, way you're dressed, you don't look like the type who could escape from a blind Sunday school teacher. You oughta be bent over a plow or slopping hogs."

Butch sent a cross-shoulder glance toward the men with him. "Josh!"

A man with a Volcanic repeating rifle sang out. "Yeah!"

"Run over to the livery. See if there's any pinto stallions. If not, describe this yahoo to Hank. Ask if he put up a horse there—any horse."

While Josh carried out the order, Butch kept Fargo covered.

"I don't like your face," he said, his voice heavy with challenge.

"Wasn't planning on selling it," Fargo replied.

"A real mouthpiece, huh? Tell me something, *Tutt*. Your hands're brown as walnuts, but your face is pale as a baby's ass. Now how can that be?"

"I wear a floppy-brim hat. Covers my face. The men in my family get moles bad if we don't."

"Yeah? Where the hell is the hat?"

"Things tend to get misplaced," Fargo replied, "when a man's hauling ass from Apaches."

Josh returned. Butch glanced at him, and the man shook his head. Butch reluctantly leathered his shooter.

"Go on about your business," he told Fargo. "But I got my eye on you."

"Why? You don't like girls?"

Josh snickered before catching himself. Butch whirled toward him, palm on the butt of his Remington. "That's real goddamn funny, ain't it?"

The man's slack face paled. "No, Butch. *Hell* no."

Butch stared at Fargo again, his eyes two burning pools of acid.

"I don't *necessarily* kill a man for a remark like that," he said. "A simple apology will keep your cowardly ass among the living."

You cocky, arrogant little bastard, Fargo thought, fuming. *That's three times now you've insulted me without cause.*

But by now dozens of people were staring at them. Exactly the kind of attention Fargo didn't need. This little piss squirt required a comeuppance, all right. But this wasn't the time or place.

Butch drummed his fingers on the butt of his gun.

"A simple apology," he repeated.

"All right," Fargo gave in, tasting bile. "Then I simply apologize."

A satisfied sneer spread across Butch's face.

"Long as we both understand who's the better man. Clear?"

The girls were watching, and that was egging Butch on. "Clear?" he repeated, raising his voice.

"Clear," Fargo said, practically choking on the word.

But as he watched Butch saunter out, his armed lick-spittles in tow, Fargo knew what was *really* clear. First he would try to pick up the trail, or whereabouts, of that arsonist and determine what he was doing in Springer.

And then he was going to settle a past-due account with a mouthy young gun tough named Butch Robinson.

5

It was just past three P.M. when a small Pueblo Indian boy knocked on the carved-oak door of the stately Robinson residence on Copper Street—the first residence in Springer built with red-clay bricks.

He asked for the master of the house and presented him with a brass emblem upon which was stamped the words SHOW ME. Nate Robinson instantly recognized the uniform insignia of the 1st Missouri Volunteers—the unit Robinson had served with as a captain in the Mexican War.

The emblem was wrapped in a crudely drawn but clear map. Robinson found his former ace artillery man camped in the lee of a well-hidden rockfall about a mile east of Springer.

Jack "Blaze" Weston had been watching and saw the man approaching. He stepped out of hiding to wait for him.

"Cap'n," he rasped out in his harsh whisper.

The simple, casual greeting startled Robinson. The tone implied they had chatted only yesterday. In fact, the two men had parted ways, down in Sonora, back in '49—their pockets bulging after two years of slaughter, rape, and plunder in the scalp-selling business.

"Blaze," Robinson replied, by habit adding one of his toothy smiles. "I see my letter caught up to you."

Robinson sat a handsome gray gelding, the saddle heavy with fancy silver trim. He had been on the verge of throwing off and shaking Weston's hand. One good look at the man's insane eyes, however, and he decided against dismounting.

Clearly Weston had deteriorated since those bloody days down in Mexico. Discreetly, Robinson unsnapped the flap of his holster.

"How you been, Blaze?" he added in a hail-fellow voice.

" 'Spect you been reading about me, Cap'n."

"That I have, that I have. Especially when you broke jail in the Arizona Territory."

"Had to. They planned to hang me."

Robinson said nothing about the charred path of senseless death and destruction that had followed Jack Weston's sick odyssey through the American West.

Instead, he stared with morbid fascination at the cause of Weston's ghoulish voice—the ugly, red, puckered flesh where he'd caught a musket ball to the throat in the thick of the battle at Cerro Gordo.

Even then, Weston, an artillery gunner, was already "touched." He earned the name Blaze because of his love for guncotton, simple but effective incendiary bombs made with cotton soaked in niter and other ingredients. He fired the pulpy, flaming bombs with deadly accuracy onto enemy positions at night, burning them to death in their sleep.

The hideous shrieks of pain from the dying Mexicans, had curled even Robinson's toes. But Weston had proved a useful crazy man, in wartime. And in peacetime, he could be a useful monster.

If he could be controlled.

Robinson glanced at his former subordinate. He wore a buckskin shirt, all right, though he also wore stiff canvas trousers tucked into narrow calfskin boots. And the cut of his beard was quite similar to that of the most wanted man in New Mexico, Skye Fargo.

"Are you aware," Robinson asked, "that another man has been mistaken for you?"

Blaze nodded. "I know who he is, too. He's tracking me."

"Jesus. Can you avoid him? I hear he's good."

"He's good," Blaze agreed. "I'm better. He won't find me. If he does, I'll kill him."

"Well, don't rush that. He's more useful to both of us while he's alive."

In fact, Skye Fargo's sudden appearance on the scene had changed all of Robinson's previous plans, which were now being made on the fly. At first he had intended to pay Blaze to torch stacks of lumber, beginning with those of Bobbie Jean's industrious older brother.

But then, after the horrific fire in Chico Springs yesterday, he began to realize his mistake. Rather than burn boards, he would have Blaze destroy board *structures*. That killed two birds with one match. It would create the impression (which Nate would encourage) that Jim Davis might well have hired Fargo to burn them down, hoping to profit off lumber sales for the rebuilding.

And of course, it meant potential sales of bricks as angry victims swore off wood.

Nate tossed the other man a chamois pouch filled with gold cartwheels. "I'd truly like there to be an unfortunate fire in Springer tonight," he said. "So we can capitalize on the sudden infamy of Fargo and the knowledge that he's in this area. You see any problem with that?"

Blaze hefted the gold, calculating its worth from long practice. Then he jammed it into a pocket without even opening the drawstring.

"No problem," he retorted in his airy, guttural voice.

"Good man. You always were the boy for sport, Blaze."

Robinson instantly regretted the remark because it opened up a window on Jack Weston's twisted mind when he replied.

"Life is a disease, Cap'n. And the only cure for it is death. The purifying death of fire is best of all."

Robinson cleared his throat, fishing for words. "Yes? Well . . . interesting theory."

He's crazy as a loon, Robinson told himself, a shudder moving up his spine.

"As I was saying," he resumed, "after the fire tonight you're going to head straight west to Taos. Take this."

Robinson handed down a map he had already drawn up.

"That'll lead you to a sawmill in the sacred valley. But right now I only want you to *look* at the place, understand? Just study it. Figure out the security and the best plan for torching it. Then stand by, that's all.

I'll get word to you if and when I want it to go up. I may decide against it if it doesn't fit my plans."

Robinson didn't want to take such a drastic action too soon. First he wanted to see how this hare-and-hound game with Fargo played out. Nate figured, if he could successfully frame Jim Davis—even arrange for a "field execution" by the Vigilance boys before Sam Rafferty returned from Santa Fe—no more action was needed.

That would eliminate the chief competition for Robinson's brick factory. The few other lumbermen in this area could be bought or chased off. But Jim Davis hated Nate and Butch Robinson on principle, and he would have to be crushed outright and forever.

Otherwise . . . simply burning his lumber stacks wouldn't be enough to stop a scrapper like Davis. It was either frame him along with Fargo or torch his sawmill. And that meant more fires, like the one he had planned for tonight, as diversions first. Events mustn't point too directly at him.

"All right," he told Blaze, "about tonight's little surprise . . ."

After Robinson had ridden out, looking carefully all around him, Weston returned to his little hidey-hole inside the rockfall. The man who was tracking him had excellent trail skills, and Blaze was moving his camp twice a day. It was old routine by now and didn't bother him a whit.

He tacked his sorrel, then tucked the big cap-and-ball Walker Colt into his red sash. Earlier, he had smeared the narrow blade of his Spanish dagger in pig manure. That way, if the blade didn't kill, the poison would. *Let* any fool find him. . . .

When breaking camp, Blaze always saved the best for last.

With trembling fingers he packed up his special fire-starting kit. Two bull's-eye canteens filled with coal oil; a square of oilskin tightly wrapped around a handful of sulfur-tipped lucifers; a doeskin pouch filled with crumbled bark and highly flammable wood fibers.

The tools of his craft.

His dead, glass-button eyes lifted to an opening in the

rocks. Across the rolling hills he could see the silhouette of Springer—including the big, boxy outline of the Queen of Sheba—traced against a bottomless blue New Mexico sky.

A den of filthy iniquity flush with sluts who let men touch their dirty dugs. Then, just because a fella's snake takes a little longer than some to get uncoiled, they mock him and say he's not a man.

Blaze would light up the sky tonight in Springer. Then he would go to Taos, as ordered. But "stand by?" Never. Eventually he would come back here, where the best was yet to be.

His reptilian eyes continued to gaze, unblinking, at the Queen of Sheba as he rubbed himself, welcoming and damning the wonderful, sinful pleasure.

All that dry, weather-sapped wood; all those slutty women.

Yes, the clock was ticking down now, for all of them.

Oh, the best was yet to be!

By the time Fargo had cleaned up in his room at the Dorsey, the sun had set and Springer was lively with the usual night sounds. He went downstairs and stepped out onto the raw lumber boardwalk, bootheels thumping loudly. Fargo liked the sound—it was hard to sneak up behind a man on boardwalks.

The Queen of Sheba was packed. Moonshine Jones spotted him and smiled slyly when Fargo headed straight through the gaudy parlor to the narrow staircase at the rear. Fargo knew Bobbie Jean's was the room at the far end of the hall—the one right over the bar, unless Moonshine was just yarning about all that "falling plaster dust" when the gal was riding her men.

"If it's Butch or Nate, go to hell!" a lilting female voice called in response to his knock.

"Neither one," Fargo assured her.

"Well then, stallion, you've got the wrong filly. The working gals are down the hall."

"The name's long-tall," Fargo reminded her through the closed door in a soft voice. "I was urged by a pretty lady in a blue dress to look her up if I ever got to Springer."

"Look her up or . . . look her over?" came the teasing response, even as Fargo heard a chair scrape back.

"Oh, I've already looked her over. That's why I'm looking her up."

A bolt shot, Fargo smelled lilac, and then Bobbie Jean Davis was framed in the doorway, hip cocked and seductively smiling. She wore only a shift of embroidered muslin, so thin her nipples clearly dinted the fabric.

"What's cookin', good-lookin'?" Fargo greeted her.

Her smile faltered for a moment as she registered his altered appearance.

"No, it's the same gorgeous blue eyes," she said, reassured. " 'Pete Helzer,' huh? Skye Fargo, are you a *fool*?"

She tugged him inside, then quickly shut and locked the door—a sturdy iron bolt, Fargo saw, approving, and a thick, solid-slab door.

The room was basic, but clean and neat with a feminine touch. A bed with a carved headboard and feather mattress, all covered by a wine red quilt with a grapevine border. There was a washstand with a pitcher and bowl, a barroom table, and two ladderback chairs.

"You *are* a fool," she decided, turning toward him. "Handsome as all get-out, shaved or bearded, but still a fool. Don't you know Butch Robinson wants to kill you? Wants it like they thirst in hell?"

"All these people who thirst in hell," Fargo replied with a grin, eyes raking her. "Tell me—do they ever *drink*?"

Fargo took all of her in, from the spun-gold tresses tumbling over slim shoulders to the pert breasts to the hourglass waist. And those moist, come-kiss-me lips— they glistened like wet rubies in the glow from wall-mounted lanterns.

"Confident, aren't you?" she said, flashing him a smile that said it wasn't a criticism.

"Plenty have tried to close my eyes," he assured her, still admiring the view. "I've learned to deal with trouble when it comes—and enjoy myself in the meantime."

"From confident to . . . cocky? Would that be a good word?" she teased, eyeing the obvious pup tent in his dungarees. "Cocky?"

"Perfect word. At the moment, *very* cocky."

She enjoyed watching him enjoy her. Bobbie Jean smoothed her hands over her thighs, deliberately drawing the fabric taut across her mons.

"Honey, you're ten times the man Butch Robinson could ever dream of being. But he's a hundred times the killer *any* man is. I've seen him do it. Killing a man is less than swatting a fly to him. His old man's the same way. Only he puts on airs and fancy St. Louis suits like he's some big muckety-muck."

She nodded toward some cards and a half-full glass on the table.

"I was playing solitaire and getting tipsy on applejack when you knocked. Thinking how this burg is *almost* as much fun as watching paint dry. Maybe tonight I'll get something a little more exciting than the usual saloon brawls and whores yelling that old lie, 'Baby, you're the *best*!' "

She pressed against Fargo, grinding her pelvis and breasts into him as their hungry, greedy tongues probed and sparred. He cupped her supple buttocks and lifted her up against the hard swell of his aroused manhood. The shift was so thin he could feel the hot dampness of her need.

She fumbled open his fly and snaked one hand inside, guiding his straining manhood to freedom.

"Oh my *God*! Honey, I do believe I just met my first three-legged man."

Her fist was pumping as she said this, and Fargo felt delicious, tickling, tingling heat in his groin.

" 'Cept one-a those legs is a little stiff . . . *oooh,* not just stiff—hard as sacked salt. Skye, it's been awhile for you, too, hasn't it?"

"Too damn long," he replied on a moan of pleasure. "I say let's do each other a nice favor."

"I agree, and *right now,*" she said, urging him on as lust made her voice husky. "Oh, God, Skye, *right now.*"

He swept her up into his arms, carried her to the bed and dropped her onto it. Fargo peeled the shift back, baring her to her tits with their hard, plum-colored nipples. While he dropped his gun belt, she spread slim, shapely thighs wide to tease him with the secret depths

49

and inner folds of her sex. Just the thought of what was coming had her pearl nubbin hard and aroused, fully exposed from under its little hood of flesh.

Fargo swung his mouth from nipple to nipple, sucking, kissing, making her gasp each time he took a little fish nibble. She was so ready for him that her inner thighs glistened, and Fargo was *past* ready before he knocked on the door.

"*Lord*, yes!" she cried out as he nudged the head of his shaft into her, adding an inch with each stroke until she had it all and was shrieking like a banshee.

"Skye, it feels like it's past my belly button," she groaned, milking all of him with her talented inner muscles.

Experience had taught Fargo that each woman, like each horse, bucked to her own pattern. That's one reason he never got tired of women and their intimate favors—it was literally a new ride each time.

And Bobbie Jean was one energetic little bucker. No matter how hard or fast Fargo thrust into her, she met the thrust and upped the ante, egging him on to more. By now the bed was hopping like a demon possessed, and they were rattling the pictures on the walls.

"There!" she cried. "*There's* the spot, oh, God, *feel* that, Skye? Don't stop, don't stop, don't stop . . . faster, faster, oh, Skye, I'm . . . *yes*, YES!"

Fargo interlaced his fingers behind her sweet derriere and lifted it right off the bed as he made his final, powerful thrusts. He took Bobbie over with him, both of them climaxing so powerfully they were left dazed and weakened for uncounted minutes.

A hard kick to the door shocked Fargo back to awareness.

He rolled off the bed, keeping Bobbie Jean protected with his body as he filled his hand with blue steel and eased back the hammer.

"Bobbie Jean? Hey, Bobbie Jean! Lemme in, why'n'cha? You need to see what you been missing, girl."

Butch Robinson. Fargo recognized the arrogant, insolent voice. Bobbie Jean rolled to the edge of the bed and pulled a scattergun out from under it. Both barrels had been sawed off to ten inches.

"Butch, you *and* your horny old man," she called to him, "can both keep grabbing my butt till Gabriel blows, it'll do you no good. If you ever come through that door, I swear half your guts will fly back out."

"You'll swallow back them words," came his surly response. "The day's coming when I'll put your ankles behind your ears."

"Piece of shit," she muttered as the sound of Butch's bootheels receded down the hallway. "Bad enough I got to live in a whorehouse to protect myself. But they won't even leave me alone here."

"Where'd you get that widow-maker, darlin'?" Fargo asked, nodding toward the sawed-off as Bobbie Jean slid it back under the bed.

"My big brother, Jimmy. He rooms at the Dorsey. He's just started a new lumber business."

"Lumber, huh?" Fargo's eyes looked thoughtful as he finished strapping on his gun belt. "So those stacks of boards at the freight office are his?"

Bobbie, sitting up in bed now, smiled with evident pride.

"His and some partners—their first big order. They've started a sawmill just west of here in the sacred valley, near Taos. Right now, he calls it just a 'one-loop outfit.' But it's a start. Won't be long, Jimmy says, he'll be able to purchase back my contract with the Robinsons."

Those soft blue eyes of hers went wistful.

"Jimmy's got his whole life invested in that sawmill and that lumber," she said. "I guess, in a way, my whole life, too."

"Just a hunch," Fargo said. "Jimmy and the Robinson men get along like cats fighting, right?"

"Why *should* they get along? Jimmy knows what they want from me. Besides, Jimmy and Nate each want the other's business."

"Interesting," Fargo muttered. "So you're an indentured servant. How the hell did you step into a mess like that?"

"Funny what you'll do when you're starving. My family was in the lumber business back in Michigan—that's how Jimmy knows the trade. We lost everything when my folks died of scarlet fever. Jimmy said we had to get out West while the demand for lumber was high. But we had no money, team, supplies, trail guide, nothing."

"I can finish the story," Fargo said. "For the price of passage west, and a way to live when you got here, you signed a contract agreeing to be a lady's maid for Cynthia Robinson?"

She nodded glumly. "I signed in 1856 in Monroe, Michigan, where they were laying over while Cynthia recovered from some illness. I've still got three long years to go. But I'll be damn lucky to make it without being raped . . . or worse."

"Worse?" Fargo repeated.

"Nate Robinson *claims* his first wife, Butch's mother, choked to death on a chicken bone. But I found an old diary she kept. She was sickly and couldn't provide 'the pleasures of the marital couch,' as she phrased it, to her husband. He was furious, threatening her, and she feared for her life."

Bobbie Jean made no claim. But Fargo caught her drift.

"Now," she continued, "Nate's got himself remarried to a 'society woman' from Baltimore. Truth is, she's a soak. A vicious, mean drunk. But she's from 'good' family. Nate can't stand her, and neither can Butch. I think she's just a gewgaw, a fancy ornament. Nate needs to look respectable and high-toned so he can control this entire territory someday."

When Fargo filtered Bobbie Jean's perspective through the lens of those "rumors" about Nate Robinson's days as a scalp-hunter, it all dovetailed.

"It's awful, being trapped under the thumb of those Robinson pigs," she added. "You met Esteban, that nice old Spanish gent who drives for them? They order him around like he's a war slave. Butch even kicks and beats him. And I keep a knife on a chain around my neck when I'm in their house. The rape *is* coming, either from Nate or Butch."

Bobbie Jean, still flushed from their lovemaking, stood up and pushed against Fargo.

"But you," she added, "can press your . . . attentions on me any time you'd like. How long you plan to stay around?"

Fargo shrugged, idly noting that the night sky beyond the room's sash windows looked oddly bright.

"Can't say," he replied. "Right now my 'plans' are being made for me by men trying to kill me."

Bobbie Jean opened her mouth to reply, but just then a man's bellowing voice roared out, like a cannon shot from the street below, "Thunderation! *FIRE!*"

6

On the frontier, a fire was every man's responsibility, even a man on the dodge. Fargo didn't bother with the stairs. With his height—and experience escaping from women's bedrooms—it was an easy matter to simply dangle from Bobbie Jean's second-story window ledge. He made sure the alley was clear below, stretched out as far as he could, and let go.

He landed on his feet, knees bending slightly to soften the impact. The entire town was painted in a lurid orange glow.

"Jesus," he whispered, staring at the roaring inferno on the western outskirts of town.

Jesus, indeed, for it was the brand-spanking new, all-lumber Methodist church. The parsonage was already totally engulfed. Even as Fargo raced toward the flames, the three-tiered belfry tower collapsed in a crackling explosion of brilliant sparks and burning embers.

"What in Sam Hill?" he heard Moonshine Jones exclaim from behind him. "How the hell could a building that size go up so quick?"

"It had professional help," Fargo called back.

Fargo and Moonshine were among the first to arrive. But by now the flames were so advanced no one could even get past the singed picket fence out front, so hot its new white paint had curled like wood shavings.

"Reverend Cunningham and his wife never had a chance," Moonshine said, bitterness edging into his tone. "You're damn right that fire was deliberate—and just guess, Mr. Dave Tutt, who they'll say set it? The famous fugitive, Skye Fargo."

Fargo didn't exactly require the reminder. Not when Butch Robinson and his vigilante thugs were bearing right down on him. Butch's glossy cavalry boots glowed like black glass in the flames.

"Real handy, ain't it, Tutt?" Butch challenged him, his right thumb caressing the walnut grip of his Remington. "You being so close by and all? Johnny-on-the-spot?"

"No closer than several of these other men," Fargo replied. "We all came out of the Queen of Sheba."

"That's thin, Tutt. I was just in the Sheba, and I didn't see you."

"Did you check in every bed upstairs?"

"You claim you was gettin' your wick dipped, huh? All right, which whore was you with?"

"A gentleman never tells."

"One more piece of your lip," Butch told him, "and we'll drag your ass through a prickly patch. I asked you which whore was you with?"

Fargo, an old hand at riling cool, began to realize he wouldn't ride this one out on the wings of a dove.

Butch's eyes narrowed at the delay, glittering hard in the rubescent glow of the inferno. "If it's caught in your craw, squaw man, hawk it up."

Let it go, Fargo cautioned himself. *Let it go. This is no damn time or place to poke at a hornet's nest.*

"Talk, you lanky bastard, or I'll rip your damn tongue out!"

That pushed Fargo past the line. He set his heels, then hit the kid with a haymaker so hard that the blow literally lifted the punk off his feet.

Butch staggered, did a slow reel, arms windmilling, and collapsed like a house of cards.

He was out cold before he hit the ground, and not likely to come to for some time. Fargo knew he shouldn't have done it. But it felt so damn good. Besides, he'd be leaving tonight, anyway—just as soon as he cut sign on the arsonist.

He shucked out his Colt and thumbed back the hammer, getting the drop on Butch's "citizens' militia" before they recovered.

"The first swinging dick who drops a bead on me,"

he warned in a tone that brooked no defiance, "will be walking with his ancestors. You boys ain't packing no stars, and that just makes you killers to me."

"Say, fellas," Moonshine interjected, "take my word for it—the only fires Dave Tutt has been setting tonight are in Bobbie Jean's tinder box."

In all the excitement of the fire, Fargo hadn't taken a close look at Moonshine. Now he realized the rail-thin bartender looked so chalk-white he was ghostly.

"Kiss my ass! That's plaster dust!" hooted one of the thugs, and they all laughed as they caught on. "Ol' Butch is out in the hallway, hard as a seed bull and beggin' her for it. And Bobbie Jean's on the other side of the door, gettin' it poured to her! Oh, Moses on the mountain, that's rich!"

"I assume you agree, boys," Moonshine added, "that's not a wise thing to tell a double-barreled asshole like Butch?"

"Mr. Tutt," said the lackey called Josh, "I enjoyed seeing you coldcock him just now, I truly did. That vicious little killer thinks he's king around here, and I only follow his orders on account I got a wife and pups on the rug. They'll die if he kills me."

The man shrugged slumping, defeated shoulders. "But . . . nothing personal. If I was you? I'd raise dust before he comes to. It's past talk now. He'll kill you deader than a Paiute grave."

Keeping his Volcanic repeater in the crook of his arm, hammer down, Josh turned and walked away, the rest following him.

Moonshine knelt and studied Butch's bloody, messed-up face.

"Damn, Fargo," he said in a whisper, "you've screwed the pooch now. Looks like you busted his snot locker in two places. It'll heal bumpy, and that vain little shit will never forget it. No way you can stay around here."

But Moonshine couldn't resist adding, his tone filled with admiration: "Damn, son, one punch knocked him sick and silly. Little bully-boy son of a bitch. If there weren't ladies gathering, I'd take a leak in his face. Him and his old man are crooked as cat shit."

Fargo wanted to ask more about that last remark. But

hanging around a bright fire, in front of a growing crowd, wasn't the best way for Fargo to ensure his old age.

The arsonist would have approached the church from that little pine woods behind it, Fargo reasoned, thus avoiding town. Just as he started to turn away, he heard a familiar voice.

"Un momento, señor?"

It was Esteban Robles.

"As I watched you handle those men just now," he said in a low voice, "I realized who you must be despite your new clothing and appearance. I suspect what you intend to do next, and *claro,* of course I want to help you. I think there is something you must know."

He glanced nervously around in the shape-shifting shadows, perhaps looking for Nate Robinson, Fargo guessed.

"When I am not driving their useless coach," he explained, scorn in his tone, "I am to pretend I am a 'footman' for these pompous *bárbaros.* I sit in the hallway, then leap up like some useless halfwit to answer each knock at the door. Today there was a small *indio* boy, he brought a secret message to Robinson."

"Hear anything?"

Esteban shook his head. "But suddenly, Robinson slipped away like a thief, even saddling his own horse. I have never seen him do such menial work. *Y ahora?* And now? Now this terrible fire, and no doubt two more souls torn savagely from life. This meeting proves nothing, but those Robinson men are both *diablos.*"

He nodded toward the bleeding man on the ground. "That one? You should kill him now for the lives it would save."

Esteban turned away, and Fargo began hooking around behind the ruined but still burning church.

Fargo's gut hunch about Nate Robinson was still just that: a hunch. But he agreed with Esteban, something was fishy about the timing of that "secret message" and this fire.

Fargo saw another complication developing in all this mess. One he hadn't found the heart to mention to Bobbie Jean so soon after doing the deed with her. But with all this wood suddenly going up in flames, it wouldn't take long for some ersatz citizen to suggest that her brother, eager for replacement orders, was bankrolling arsonist Skye Fargo.

Once again Fargo's confident enemy had taken no pains, at first, to cover his trail in or out from the scene of his heinous crime.

Just the opposite—clearly he wanted Fargo to trail him.

About fifty feet behind the church, the Trailsman quickly confirmed that the same killer was at work by studying the clear dirt patterns left on the ground by boots with hobnailed soles. Same as the prints in the alley in Chico Springs.

Fargo decided to check the killer's back-trail first, to confirm an important hunch. He knew the arsonist had escaped headed due west. Only Taos Pueblo lay in that direction, and slightly south of there, the smaller pueblo of Ranchos de Taos. That trail would be easy enough to find, but Fargo still needed to know where the sick son of a bitch had camped.

Because there was truth in the smallest signs.

Truth that pointed a good scout like Fargo toward not just the killer—but also toward the well-dressed citizens who hired him. Both species of roach required crushing.

Moonshine Jones caught him before he left and handed him a canteen of cold coffee, then some tortillas and a hunk of salt meat wrapped in cheesecloth.

"I think it's a fool's errand," Moonshine admitted. "But best of luck, Mr. Fargo. I know you have to go after him to clear your own name. I also suspect, however, that by now you know who this must be?"

"Know it?" Fargo shook his head. "I know who you mean, sure. But there's plenty like him loose in the country. At this point, all I know for sure is he ain't *me*. Thanks for the rations."

The killer's back-trail headed east, and Fargo was able to reunite with his well-rested stallion without swinging wide and losing the trail. Within an hour, he was carefully searching the killer's rock-nest camp, now clearly deserted.

Same scraps of ash-pone, same tobacco spit. It was easy to establish that two horses had been in the area, one tethered for long hours, the other ridden for only one brief visit—the rider hadn't even dismounted.

It was those prints Fargo studied closely with an experienced eye, putting his cheek right on the ground and even using a precious sulfur match for a better look. He could closely estimate how recently hoofprints were made by how much of the grass had started to spring back up inside them.

This lone rider had visited the killer about five or six hours ago. By Fargo's reckoning, that was about the same time he had spotted Nate Robinson returning to town from this direction.

"Still ain't proof," he said absently, but even the Ovaro looked skeptical by now.

The part Nate and Butch were playing, if any, would have to wait. Right now the mad arsonist was on the loose, probably heading for Taos.

Again Fargo had little trouble picking up the first leg of his quarry's escape path. But just as he had the last time, Fargo's skillful enemy used every clever dodge known to trail-craft.

There were false trails made to look real, real trails made to look false; sometimes the trail disappeared into thin air, as if the man's horse had simply sprouted wings.

But the climax for Fargo was the full hour he spent traveling in the wrong direction when his wily enemy snookered him by nailing his horse's shoes on backwards!

And now a new twist had been added to the deadly game—little "surprises" to taunt Fargo. He was urging the Ovaro up out of a shallow creek when he spotted an old leather musette bag—of the shoulder-strap type carried by soldiers on a long march—lying among the reeds along the bank.

Fargo threw off and knelt to study it before poking it cautiously with a stick. He carefully lifted the leather cover flap, and suddenly venom-dripping fangs launched straight at his throat!

Only the survival reflexes of a cat saved him. The

fangs missed him, the rattlesnake's dry scales scraping his neck, and seconds later the serpent was pinned under Fargo's Arkansas Toothpick.

"He cut off the damn rattles," Fargo marveled aloud. "Moonshine had it right. This is a fool's errand."

But just then he remembered Antonio Two Moons' grief-stricken words spoken over the charred remains of Elena Vargas: *How long must her soul now hover in torment?*

Fargo stepped into a stirrup and swung up into leather. A little squeeze of his knees, and man and horse pressed on into the long night, bearing toward the distant, dark spine of the Taos Mountains.

And bearing toward a monster spawned in the bowels of hell.

"You know me, all of you," Jemez Gray Eyes told his band. "I have killed Comanches, Mexican lancers, and the yellow-legged soldiers. But *that* one?"

Jemez nodded toward a lone rider far below their position in the mountain rimrock. The man and his sorrel were a silent shadow gliding across the moonlit terrain.

"That one," the Mescalero repeated, "is one to let alone. A fire demon. He is marked as one who is unclean and lives by *ánti.*"

His use of that forbidden and evil word, even among this band of hard, outcast raiders, shocked the rest into uncomfortable silence. *Ánti,* the evil inspired directly by the Most Low—so evil that even talking about it might curse one for life.

"Jemez speaks straight words," said Hoyero, his lieutenant, who took his name from the mountain branch of the Jicarillas. "I am a man who fears little—in *this* world. And I will die cursing my enemy. True, I no longer sing or dance or put up prayer plumes. But I believe in Usen, the Giver of Life. And brothers?"

Hoyero jumped down off his observation rock and met each man's eyes in the moonlight before speaking again.

"In the year the white man's winter-count calls 1848, the pale ones drove out the brown ones but continued the war on us Fighting-Men. So? I will fight them also."

Hoyero pointed in the direction of the rider.

"But that one below? There was a time, down south of Apacheria, when I looked into that one's eyes. I lost all courage, for I had gazed directly into the eyes of he whose name may not be said."

Jemez and Hoyero, being good fighters and admired orators, were natural leaders among a people who had never had much love for authority. Zunis and foreigners called them Apache, "enemy," a word they liked. But they called themselves by the ancient name, the Fighting-Men.

"*Let* this white demon rage," Jemez said. "*Let* him burn to ashes these whiteskins and Mexicans and these cowardly, dirt-scratching 'red men' who now worship a virgin they claim had a child."

Jemez, like all the rest, wore a headband to clear the thick, long hair from his vision. He was a Pecos river Mescalero by birth, a nomadic outcast by choice. He swept an arm out, indicating the populated mountains surrounding them.

"We are well north of our usual mescal cactus country, this is true. But the raiding is easy here in these mountain villages. The bluecoat soldiers are lazy, and so are their useless horses. The soldiers do not want to die just to return some old man's mule or some Indian village's grain harvest."

The others nodded agreement. Jemez and his group of outcasts were always hungry, but never starving. No troop of soldiers could catch them, and woe to any who drew too close. The band raided for everything they had—clothing, food, horses, weapons. Otherwise, survival in this harsh land meant constant and menial work. Women's work beneath the dignity of the Fighting-Men.

"Let this evil one kill *all* the hair-face invaders and their praying Indians," Jemez scoffed. "Do not forget, Usen can use evil to His own good purpose. But this other one—the man the Navajos call Son of Light—he means to kill the fire demon. He will need watching."

"He has a fine stallion," Hoyero added. "One I like. So perhaps Son of Light will require more than mere watching. Perhaps he will require killing."

* * *

Once again it was dark, and Skye Fargo was in his saddle instead of his bedroll.

The trail he was following entered a series of connecting canyons of coarse-grained metamorphic rock. Even in this dim light, alternating layers of minerals—feldspar, quartz, mica—gave the rock walls a banded appearance.

By sunrise he crested a long spine and got an excellent view of Taos Pueblo. It was set like a gem in the sacred valley, the Taos mountains looming all around. Already, there was a brilliant blue sky overhead. The surrounding pastures were alive with wild iris, and the fences were covered with plum blossoms.

Even as the yellow-orange ball of sun rose higher over the sacred valley, Fargo rode cautiously into the center of Taos plaza. The place was still mostly silent except for a lonely dog that wouldn't stop howling.

St. Vrain's General Store dominated the south side of the plaza, thick wooden shutters with gun ports covering the windows. Most of the pueblo's window facings and doors were painted "Taos blue"—the color of turquoise. "Skystone" was the Indian word for their beloved stone.

"Desayuno, señor?"

The speaker was on old *indio* woman wrapped in a faded *manta,* offering to sell him some breakfast.

Fargo was busy trying to sort his quarry's fresh prints out from the confusion in the dusty plaza. He had rations, thanks to Moonshine, but he swung down and bought a bowl of simple cornmeal gruel to put something hot in his belly.

"Have you seen a man ride past this morning?" Fargo asked her in Spanish. "A bearded man in buckskins?"

"Mal ojo," she muttered, making the sign to ward off the evil eye and shooing him away.

Fargo took that as a yes and began to worry anew. It was the old cat-and-mouse game, and this time Fargo sure as hell wished he felt more like the cat. But he couldn't—not with this one.

Moonshine's voice, repeating in memory: *By now you know who this must be?*

Fargo had denied it. But, in truth, with that first, hor-

rific death scream in Chico Springs, a name had been . . .
emblazoned in his thoughts.

And dread now lay heavy in his stomach, like greasy
food that wouldn't digest. Dread, and the fear even
brave men feel when they might, at any moment,
glimpse the grinning face of Satan.

"C'mon, boy, let's chance a feed," Fargo decided,
glancing around the sleepy plaza. News was always slow
to reach Taos, anyway, and Fargo noticed there was only
a *mozo* at the livery, a young Mexican boy who assisted
the owner.

"Curry him good, *chico*," Fargo told the kid. He
flipped him four bits American. "Grain him, too, *'sta
bien*? Crushed barley, if you got it."

"*Sí, jefe.*"

Fargo moved back out into the street, his neck sweat-
ing despite the cool morning breeze. He could feel the
killer's mocking eyes tracking him.

There were also signs of more people and activity.
Pueblo Indians tanning hides and weaving their beautiful
blankets, grinding corn and feeding chickens. But no one
seemed to much notice this tall, lean-hipped, blue-eyed
Anglo with the dark beard stubble.

Why would they? Taos was a longtime crossroads
spot, used to the likes of Kit Carson, Charles Bent, Al-
bert Pike, Uncle Dick Wootton. Fargo himself had
shaken the hand of Padre Antonio Jose Martinez, whose
El Crepusculo was the first newspaper west of the
Mississippi.

But as he again sorted out the one set of prints he'd
been following, made distinctive by a chipped left rear
shoe, Fargo knew a killer had invaded Taos—a madman
bent on raw, savage destruction and pain.

The tracks led through the plaza, then into an alley
between a row of adobe houses.

Fargo, feeling his pulse quicken, drew steel.

But the alley was clear. Fargo was halfway through it
when he spotted the old, yellowed newspaper clipping.
It had been left right over one of the hoofprints,
weighted down with a rock.

Fear gripping his throat, Fargo read the headline:

TWENTY-SEVEN ORPHANS KILLED IN
'SUSPICIOUS' OMAHA INFERNO!!!

The shock of final certainty iced Fargo's blood. He didn't bother reading the story. Didn't have the stomach for it because he already knew the details. That horrific fire, several years back, had been blamed on America's most notorious arsonist.

And this mocking clue confirmed what Fargo had feared all along: He was on the trail of Jack "Blaze" Weston.

In Fargo's view, Weston was the lowest living murderer in America. More than three-dozen known fires to his "credit." A man about whom little was know because he lived in the margins and shadows and mixed with few men. Even his name could be a lie—he had been arrested in Arizona Territory, wearing a silver belt buckle with the name etched into it. But he had escaped.

There was a scratching noise behind Fargo. He whirled, lunging to one side as he tried to spot his target.

Which turned out to be a cat burying its waste.

"Nerve up, old son," Fargo ordered himself, resuming the trail through the alley. "The waltz is only beginning."

Fargo took five more cautious steps through the alley. When he saw what was written in the sand, a cold tongue licked down his spine.

ORPHANS *PREFERRED*, FARGO!

"This shit's for the birds," a worried Nate Robinson told his son.

Nate tapped a Western Union message protruding from the breast pocket of his vermilion jacket.

"This is a report from Steve Kitchens at Taos. Weston's been there, all right. But he hardly spent any time at all watching the sawmill operation like I told him to do. Now he's evidently off on his own little mad romp to the south. Steve's good at scouting and trailing and such, but he can't make sense of Weston's plans."

"The hell you expect?" Butch shot back. "Bastard's mad as a March hare. It was a fool's play to hire him."

Nate knew his son was a jackass, which only made it taste more bitter to admit he'd begun to suspect the same thing about Blaze himself—the man *was* dangerously insane. In fact, he wanted to turn his horse and flee the moment he stared into those murderous eyes yesterday. But greed made him stay.

"Shit," Butch hissed, gingerly touching his nose.

A plaster cast made it twice its normal size. Butch had stretched out on a fancy white brocade couch. "Resting up," as he put it, from the iron-fisted blow last night that would leave his nose disfigured for life. In truth, he was ashamed to show himself in front of the men. But that shame was slowly turning to a boiling rage aimed squarely at Skye Fargo.

Both men spoke in low tones so that Bobbie Jean and Esteban, working nearby in the house, wouldn't overhear them.

"Tell you this much," Butch added, "you best hope

like hell *our* names don't get linked to that crazy son of a bitch. 'Magine what it's like when the hangman snugs that big old knot under your ear. They say some men piss themselves even before the trap springs open. Some even—"

"The hell's got into you?" Nate snapped. "A man can't go puny once the attack is under way. Anyhow, nobody saw me with him, and I paid in gold."

"Yeah, see there? You *think* about that, old man. You already gave him the money! Hell, why not give him a whack at your wife while you're at it? Face it. He's gonna break it off inside us."

Nate shook his head. As usual he was tailored to the image of success. He wore a morning suit and a fancy-stitched shirt with genuine pearl snaps on the cuffs—an image he felt befitting for a soon-to-be mandarin of the New Mexico Territory.

"You're right that Blaze is insane," Nate conceded. "And a cold-blooded killer. But there's a strange . . . honor to the man. He was that way when I knew him in the Army, and I think he still is. He'll keep his word—after his own fashion."

Nate paused, idly scratching at one of the drooping Icadilly Weepers framing his cheeks like scruffy silver fur.

"Nonetheless," he admitted, "talk about a loose cannon. I told Steve to run his traps, see what he can find out about Weston's whereabouts. Luckily, through Steve, I've cultivated some good contacts in Taos."

Nate paced the fancy parlor's rose-patterned carpet, his expression preoccupied. Just east of here, in Texas, the cotton and cattle hierarchy was already in place. But Nate saw a future in manufacturing, not ranching or agriculture. It was the industrial revolution, with its belching smokestacks, that fueled wealth.

His brickyard was only the seedling. Before he died, his factories would dominate Santa Fe and its cheap labor pool of poor Indians. It was easy to acquire power if you got in early and grabbed a big hunk of the bonanza.

But you *kept* your fortune, built on it, by disguising

true motives with deceptive manners and false rhetoric. And by destroying your competition with one hand extended in friendship and the other behind your back, holding a knife.

"The hell you find worth grinning about?" Butch carped.

"You know my philosophy, Butchie boy. If a man knows exactly how much money he's worth, he's not all that wealthy yet. *Rich,* m'lad, is when you have so damn much money you can't even tote it up. And, damn it, I know *exactly* how much I've got."

In his strong feeling, Nate's voice had carried. Bobbie Jean was on the second-floor landing, combing out some falls and wigs for Cynthia Robinson and detesting every second of it. Esteban had been put to work polishing the stair rail of antique brass.

Bobbie Jean's fetching face scrunched into a smirk at Nate's so-called "philosophy."

"I know exactly how much he's got, too," she muttered sarcastically to Esteban. "Why do you think his woman is always so cranky?"

Esteban caught his laughter just in time—Butch had aimed suspicious eyes in their direction.

"But once I gain control of the town-site charter," Nate went on confidently, "good-bye and amen, brother! It's all this goddamn law pushing in everywhere now. Lawyers, U.S. marshals, circuit judges, territorial prisons. Hell. It was wide open back in the days when this region was part of the Spanish land-grant country."

"Must have been some *hair-raising* days back then, eh, Nathaniel?" came Cynthia Robinson's most emasculating voice, from the doorway of the connecting parlor. It was only late morning, and she was already flushed from tipping her flask.

Bobbie Jean and Esteban exchanged surprised glances. So Nate's "high-society" wife *had* somehow heard the rumors?

"And now," Cynthia added with barbed scorn, "he means to join the Beacon Hill elite."

Nate was only momentarily nonplussed.

"They always talk who never think, my dear. I'm what

you call a forward-oriented man," he assured her. "Where money is involved there's no such thing as hypocrisy. The profit motive evolved *before* ethics."

"*Cristo,*" Esteban muttered to Bobbie Jean. "The man has . . . *cómo se dice?* True skill with a cliché."

But Esteban spoke too loudly, and Butch had keen hearing. He sat up suddenly.

"The hell's bitin' at you, dago?" he called to the old man.

Esteban only shook his head, busy polishing a rail. *Ay, Dios!* If only he were a younger man. Then at least he could flee up to Colorado and top sugar beets for a humble living.

"Somethin' caught in your craw?" Butch forced the issue.

"Jesus, Butch, pick on someone your own age," Bobbie Jean snapped. "He was talking to me—just asking if I've seen the new medicine show in town, that's all."

Butch's surly tone softened as he eyed the swell of Bobbie Jean's bodice.

"Well, the old fart ain't s'posed to be talking," he groused. "He's earning his keep."

"Speaking of that," Nate said, "the hell you doing lazing around this late in the day? This drifter Dave Tutt got you treed? Scared to leave the house now?"

Butch pushed to his feet this time, face twisted with rage.

"Pitch it to hell! Dave Tutt, my lily-white ass. *Ain't* no goddamn Dave Tutt, I tell you. That was Skye Fargo who coldcocked me last night. The second time now. Just blindsided me, the low-crawling coward."

"You don't know it's Fargo."

"Like hell I don't!"

Nate waved a careless hand. "All right, so what if it was Alexander the Great? It's damn near noon. If you can't put a few hours into the business, you should at least be out riding with the rest of the boys, upholding justice. You're their dead aim."

"Yeah? Well, you can pitch all that to hell, too," Butch said hotly. "I was laid out cold for an hour! Hell, my head's pounding like a tom-tom."

Nate's hard, obsidian eyes mocked his puling whelp.

"Son, you're some pumpkins with a barking iron, I'll grant that. Makes me proud, too. But you got no fighting fettle, boy. I've rode with lead in me, blood spurting out in ropes."

"Yeah, yeah, you were the big he-bear, old man, back when Noah built the ark."

Butch said this with little interest. His mood had turned especially foul now that Fargo's name had come up. He needed to fly into a rage, and he needed a target.

"*You*, Don Dumbshit!" he shouted up at Esteban. "Fire up some lamps, goddamnit, or else yank open some drapes! I can't see a mother-loving thing in here."

"Mother-loving," Cynthia's voice repeated through the door. "Oh, that's rich!"

"You're indisposed, dear," Nate said in a quiet tone devoid now of any politeness. "Go rest."

"You two disgust me," she said, slamming the door.

Nate, fingering the heavy brass studding on his belt, glanced around to make sure Bobbie Jean and Esteban couldn't hear him. He lowered his voice.

"How 'bout the other business?" he hinted to his son. "With Davis?"

"Yeah, that." Butch sat down again, still tenderly touching his nose. "Ray Nearhood and Danny Appling are taking care of it later today," he replied. "We bribed a Mexer maid at the Dorsey. She's gonna 'find' the stuff in Jimmy's room and report it to the Vigilance Committee."

"Like any good, concerned citizen would." Nate approved this with a nod. "What are they planting?"

"Kerosene, rags, tinder. Even better—we'll be putting a list in Davis' room, writ in his hand, of the big wooden structures in this area. It was just a, whatchamacallit, a customer list Danny and Josh stole from his little office beside the freight yard. But we'll cut that part off. Make it seem like he had a list of buildings he meant to torch."

"That'll sell newspapers," Nate said. "Better and better. But remember, all that only gets him arrested. Davis is well-enough liked around town. And Sam Rafferty is due back soon."

Butch nodded. "And Rafferty might be tough as boar bristles, but he's also fair. Besides, he likes Jimmy. He'll release him unless there's better evidence."

"My point exactly. So we'll have to move quick once he's locked up. He's going to be killed trying to escape. And then, there goes our major competition."

"There's still that cousin of his and their crew at the sawmill," Butch pointed out.

"What, Lon Brubaker? He and the rest are good workers, sure. But Jimmy's the brains behind the operation, the popular one who hustles the orders. Besides, with Jimmy pegged for a woman-killing, preacher-roasting arsonist, nobody'll do business with them anyway."

"Which still leaves two problems, way I size it," Butch said. "Blaze Weston and Skye Fargo. Blaze once took orders from you and you claim he will still, so he's your headache. But Skye goddamn Fargo is all mine, and I mean to plug him slow and painful, make him bleed out for hours."

Fargo, feeling like a marked man, slowly dogged Blaze Weston's trail. Or tried to—Weston had left so *many* trails that Fargo felt like a hound trying to catch four rabbits.

This one eventually seemed to lead south, and before long Fargo's ears picked up the unmistakable, shearing racket of a steam saw biting into thick timber. The sound spooked the Ovaro at first, but he quickly accepted it when his master did also.

Fargo's hunch about Nate and Butch Robinson was back, only by now it was changing from a hunch to a near certainty.

Fargo cleared a copse of trees and spotted the sawmill, a crude operation with only about six workers he could see. It was located in a thickly forested pocket of the sacred valley, halfway between Taos Pueblo and Ranchos de Taos, a separate little adobe village four miles south.

Huge stacks of freshly milled lumber, under armed guard, occupied a ridge behind the sawmill. Fargo rode toward the guard, raising one hand high in the universal frontier sign to show his intentions were peaceful.

"Howdy."

The guard met his greeting with a wary but civil nod. He was about forty, balding, with a lumpy chin. Since his visitor was alone and it was broad daylight, he kept his shotgun pointed toward the ground.

"Guarding Jimmy's lumber, huh?" Fargo said.

"Not just Jimmy's, stranger. Mine, too. I'm Lon Brubaker, Jimmy's cousin on his ma's side. And them 'jacks felling trees and milling the boards—either cousins or friends of ours who were in the lumber trade back in Michigan. We come out one by one as Jimmy built the business up from pure air."

He spoke with evident pride. The pride of a hard, honest worker who now finally had a little something of his own.

Fargo nodded. "And everything you folks got is tied up in this sawmill?"

Wariness crept back into Brubaker's sunburned face. " 'At's right. Matter fact, I'd sooner lose all my jaw teeth than even one board. Say, mister . . ." The gun didn't come up, but suspicion hardened his face. "Just who are you, anyhow?"

"Name's Dave Tutt," Fargo lied, figuring that summer name couldn't have reached Taos yet.

"And you say you're a friend of Jimmy's? I sure never met you before."

"Never said I knew Jimmy. Actually, I know his sister."

A little grin played on Brubaker's chapped lips. "Know her in the Old Testament sense?"

Fargo's diplomatic silence answered for him.

"You'd be Bobbie Jean's type," Brubaker said. "Hey, hold on . . . just remembered something about her. She only goes for men over six feet, like you. And she's got a special name for 'em."

"Call me long-tall," Fargo said solemnly, and Brubaker enjoyed a laughing fit.

" 'Cept I didn't know," Fargo added, frowning, "it was a universal name."

Brubaker winked. "You're all long-tall to her, and you're all the best. You know how women are."

Fargo sighed. "Seems I learn more every day, dammit."

"Pull up a rock, Dave," Brubaker invited.

Fargo swung down and let the Ovaro graze pine needles. If Lon had noticed the stallion and wondered anything about him, he didn't show any suspicion. Fargo explained that he was on the trail of the arsonist, and that it led right here.

"Jesus," Brubaker said, casting a nervous glance around. "Last I heard, he was in Springer."

"He was until he torched a church there last night. Like the wind, he gets around. Seen anybody at all poking around here?"

Brubaker scratched his chin, thinking about it. "Nobody that don't belong around here. I did think it was strange, though, that Steve Kitchens rode past here earlier. Several times."

"Who's he?"

"Lives in Taos, but gets around this entire area plenty. Works for Nate Robinson. Sort of a jack-of-all-trades. Rides guard on brick shipments and whatnot."

Whatnot. That could include reporting on Nate Robinson's newest "employee," Blaze Weston. Fargo nodded, not surprised by the news.

"Stay alert," Fargo warned the guard. "Especially after dark. The man we're up against is Blaze Weston, and right now he's probably watching both of us."

Brubaker turned so pale it looked like he'd been leeched.

"Blaze Wes—? You *gotta* be shitting me!"

"Nope. Got proof."

"But everybody's saying it's some jasper called Skye Fargo. Also called the Trailsman. I ain't been out here long enough to know about him."

"Believe me," Fargo said as he took up the reins again, "that's a mistaken-identity problem. The man prowling New Mexico with matches in his hand is Blaze Weston. I plan to hound him into hell, keep him on the run in hopes he can't torch anything else. But trying to lay hands on him is like trying to strangle a jellyfish."

Fargo rode on again, eyes missing nothing. Only after painstaking scouting, he picked up Weston's trail.

It seemed to lead in circles around the sawmill, either to pester Fargo or because Weston wanted to study the area. In any case, Weston hadn't remained long before the trail turned south again.

Then north.

Then east.

Then west before again jogging south.

Fargo, weary from climbing in and out of leather to examine signs, cast a frustrated sigh.

"Tell it to you straight, old campaigner," he said to his Ovaro, "*this* wily son of a bitch has got me chasing my own tail."

The afternoon heated up as the sun rose higher. Fargo forded the Rio Grande about three hours ride southwest of Ranchos de Taos.

By now, at least he had a solid trail to follow. His quarry had tired of the cat-and-mouse game, at least for the moment. But the rough mountain path was sandy and rocky in places with washouts that had to be detoured.

Fargo was in mostly forested mountains now. But now and then the tree cover thinned, and he pulled down his hat against the swirling dust storms that plagued much of New Mexico, especially in late afternoon.

He could glance over his shoulder and glimpse the Pecos river. It rose through the Sangre de Cristo range, frothing and twisting its way southward to eventually become the pathetic desert ditch known as the Pecos Stream.

But not one actual glimpse, since this strange odyssey began three days earlier in Chico Springs, of Blaze Weston. Everywhere felt, nowhere seen.

The trail led Fargo into the remote mountain village of La Paz. Nerves taut, Fargo knocked the riding thong off the Colt's hammer and loosened the Henry in its boot. Then he rode slowly through the village, expecting an ambush at any moment. His eyes studied everything, yet stayed in motion.

The few dwellings were of puddled adobe, the Indian style, with layers of grass-impregnated mud poured between forms, drying one layer on the other. Even this poor excuse for a village had its solid adobe church with thick, buttressed walls.

But the town itself seemed like a graveyard. At first he noticed no one, and the only sound came from an old, rotting windlass creaking like a rusty hinge in the breeze.

Nobody in sight. How could that be . . . unless some-thing, or some*one*, had frightened them into hiding.

He remembered the old woman in Taos Plaza, turning away as if from the face of evil itself when he'd asked if she'd seen a rider earlier.

Sweat broke out on Fargo's temples. The Ovaro's hoof-clops echoed eerily as the Trailsman rode through the virtual ghost village. Yellow plumes of dust rose be-hind them, floating a long time in the warm, still air. Fargo's eyes, shaded under his hat, stayed in constant motion, with special attention to the best ambush points.

The village was too small for a feed stable (though not for an undertaker's parlor, he noticed). When he was safely through town, Fargo swung down and quickly tossed his saddle and pad aside. He spread the sweat-saturated saddle blanket out to dry off a bit in the hot sun. Otherwise, he risked chilling his horse when the sun went down and the mountain wind took on a knife edge.

A gut bag tied to Fargo's saddle horn bulged with water. He quickly rubbed the sweat off his stallion, then watered him from his hat—just a few swallows as a promise of more to come.

The Ovaro's ears suddenly pricked forward in a warn-ing sign Fargo had long ago learned to respect.

Even as he hurled himself to the ground, Fargo spot-ted a human form and motion from the corner of one eye.

With a solid *thwack,* a broad-bladed Spanish dagger embedded itself deeply into the bole of a tree—just be-hind the exact spot where Fargo had been standing a heartbeat earlier.

Fargo rolled fast and hard, taking cover behind a hum-mock. He filled his hand. Desperately, he raised and lowered his head, seeking a bead.

Nothing.

He'll shoot my horse, Fargo suddenly worried. The Ovaro stood fully exposed, alerted but unsure what the danger was. Nor did he want to flee without Fargo.

Knowing it could happen at any moment, Fargo preferred any action over none. He snapped off a round well over the Ovaro's head, sending the pinto bolting into tree cover.

But the hummock was a poor hiding place, and Fargo provided a momentary target when he lifted his arm to fire. Only a second after his shot, a booming explosion sent a lead ball hurling into the hummock, tearing out a fist-sized chunk and raining dirt into Fargo's face.

"There!" Fargo muttered triumphantly when he spotted a blue curl of smoke. It rose from a clump of bushes in front of a rock shelf about thirty feet away.

Finally, a damn target! Not Weston himself yet, but his general location—and that was at least something to shoot at.

And shoot Fargo did, on the fast roll, peppering that spot with all six beans in the wheel. Sparks flew when his bullets chipped the flint rocks behind the bushes.

When his hammer clicked on the firing pin, he rolled into a little swale and reloaded. But even before he snapped shut the Colt's loading gate, Fargo heard the rapid drumbeat of escaping hooves.

His own mount was stripped of tack. Besides, Blaze Weston was one man Fargo had no desire to go rushing headlong after.

That sentiment was only reinforced when Fargo got a closer look at that dagger and realized the blade was poisoned with feces. Even a flesh wound and Fargo would have died, screaming in agony, twenty-four hours later.

But now, for the first time, he had flushed his quarry out and had him on the run.

"*Dios mío*, please help me to live a live of piety," prayed a pretty *mestiza* as Blaze watched her from hiding, his excited breath whistling in his nostrils.

He listened to the Spanish words, liking the sound of them in the still morning air.

"*Quiero vivir una vida de fe.*"

Blaze knew the words, all right. She was asking God to help her live a life of faith. Piety, faith . . . the damned beautiful little siren! Trying to smother the fire in her loins with a blanket of religion.

"Quiero vivir una vida de devoción."

Yeah, Blaze thought, *sure you want to lead a devout life, you little* puta. *That's why you're standing there half-naked—so you can get some man all het up.*

The woman's abundant beauty had struck Blaze with physical force the first moment he saw her after sneaking into her mountain village on foot. In this sleepy, modest little place she stood out like a brass spittoon in a funeral parlor.

She had the best features of Mexican and Indian blood. Wide, coffee-brown eyes were set like gems behind delicate yet prominent cheekbones. Flawless, honey-colored skin offset raven black hair pulled back into a chignon.

"Dios mío, quiero vivir una vida de amor."

Oh, I bet you get plenty of "amor," *all right, you flaunting little piece,* Blaze fumed silently. *Men stick their things in her hole, and the devil could slip in with them.*

It was just after sunrise. He had been riding hard all night to build a lead on Fargo. Now he had arrived in Santa Cruz, just a little flyspeck on the trail north of Santa Fe. A sleepy little adobe and mud Indian pueblo, one of dozens dotting the Rio Grande valley.

And then Fate led his eyes to *her*.

He had watched her emerge from her adobe home and circle around to a little seep spring behind it. She wore a pretty white cotton dress with black trim.

Even as Blaze watched from the surrounding trees, she had removed her light fawn-skin moccasins.

Then she slid the dress over her head and left it in a puddle on the ground. Bare naked, her breasts swaying like lake swells, she waded out into the pool.

Blaze stared at the big, chocolate-colored nipples, all stiff and pointy in the morning chill of the water. How could she stand there boldly naked like that and *pray*? She didn't even seem ashamed, as if the naked body were something natural!

"Dear God," called her soft, musical voice, "please give me the strength to live one day at a time."

Blaze began to sneak back to his horse, thinking, *One day at a time is all she'll need because one day is all she has left.*

By long habit Blaze avoided the town street, sneaking behind houses. Even in the Army he had never felt comfortable in the company of others.

He pitched a cold camp off the trail, using his saddle for a pillow. Blaze never slept longer than thirty minutes at a time—survival, for him, meant constantly moving on. Captain Robinson had told him to just stand pat in Taos. But Fargo made that impossible. So now Fargo would soon regret that he ever started this personal vendetta.

Before he stretched out, Blaze pulled the big cap-and-ball Walker Colt from his sash and made sure the powder load hadn't clumped. Then he laid it beside his saddle.

Tonight, he told himself as he tumbled over the threshold into sleep.

The night was his time. And the pretty little *mestiza* would be purified.

8

On the trail east of Santa Cruz, a bone-weary Skye Fargo paused to let a freight wagon rattle past, sideboards straining.

"Whoa, you ugly animules!" the teamster called out, pushing the brake lever with his foot.

The driver, stinking from a long ride, offered Fargo a bottle of cheap forty-rod.

"Mister, I'm pure people-starved," he greeted Fargo. "Been talking to mules all day. Spot of the giant killer? No offense, but you look like you could use a jolt."

"Truer words, and all that," Fargo said gratefully as he accepted the bottle.

Damn straight he could use a bracer, Fargo told himself, after the night he just survived. In fact, he took two deep swallows that heated his empty belly.

Vigilantes had spotted him and the Ovaro, just before sunset yesterday, and Fargo had been forced to spend a night holed up in a bear's den, hoping like hell the usual tenant didn't appear.

Now night was coming on, and Blaze Weston had gotten a day's reprieve from the pressure of pursuit. An entire day to pick his next victim, plan his next pyrotechnic nightmare.

"'Preciate it," he said, handing the bottle back. "Headed to Santa Fe?"

"'City of the Holy Faith,' yessir. And thank God there's more sin than faith."

The teamster hooked a thumb over his shoulder. "Hauling furniture from Springer."

"Springer, huh? What's the news back there?"

"Methodist church was burned to ashes two days ago. Killed the preacher and his wife. And, damnedest thing—right 'fore I left yestiddy Jimmy Davis was locked up for it."

Fargo kept the surprise out of his face. "Davis? I thought Skye Fargo was s'posed to be the arsonist."

"The vigilante bunch claim the two of 'em must be in cahoots."

"Nate Robinson's really pushing that, hey?"

The driver nodded.

"They got him in jail?" Fargo asked.

"Sure, and I hear he got worked over pretty good, too, for 'resisting arrest.' Bobbie Jean's taking it hard. Her brother seems like a good jake to me. He just better hope Sheriff Rafferty gets back soon."

He'll be dead by the time that happens, Fargo told himself, his mind already scheming what the hell to do about it.

The wagon rolled on, and Fargo continued tracking the elusive Blaze Weston. The trail led straight toward the ancient Indian village of Santa Cruz, tucked away in the shadow of the Sangre de Cristo range.

So far Fargo had seen no more signs of those Apaches. But when you couldn't see them was the time to worry most. An Apache's main religious rite, in Fargo's experience, was praying his enemy into the ground.

Fargo already had enough threat from the sickness of Blaze Weston. At times, especially on lower slopes far from water, the green thinned out to scrub cottonwoods and mesquite. That left Fargo vulnerable, and across such expanses he kicked the Ovaro up to a lope.

It was dark when Fargo rode in. These villages were isolated from the news in Anglo towns like Springer and Chico Springs, so he didn't worry about his stallion tipping anyone off.

The village was still and silent, with burnished gold light spilling through open doorways and windows. For a moment, just at the edge of the pueblo, Fargo felt a shudder pass through the Ovaro.

The wind, slicing off the Sangre de Cristo, suddenly rose to a shriek that pressed the grass flat. Fargo felt the hair on his arms stiffen.

Blaze was here or he'd been here lately, all right. The stink of his evil stained the very air.

Fargo was halfway through the little pueblo, eyes and ears cocked like the Colt in his hand.

He was sick of eating tortillas and salt meat. Fargo remembered there used to be a flyblown cantina, at the far edge of the village, where a man could get liquor and hot grub, if he didn't mind picking the roaches out of his food.

Moonshine Jones had slipped Fargo some money, but he lost most of it in his flight from the vigilantes. Now he was damn near strapped, down to U.S. Script—soldiers' money that many folks were reluctant to accept, especially this far from big towns.

Fargo was passing an adobe hovel when a young *mestiza* emerged, carrying an *olla,* a clay water jar, on her hip. She looked pretty in a white dress with black trim.

Their eyes met. In that flattering light she was just about the prettiest sight Fargo had seen in a long while.

"Muy buenas noches," she greeted him shyly.

"Qué hay de nuevo?" he called back.

She giggled at her own forwardness and the fact that she wasn't bothered by the way his eyes flowed over her, taking her measure and liking it.

Before she hurried behind her house for water, she gave him a quick and uncertain smile—the restive smile of a woman harboring secret ambitions.

A beauty like that has gotta have a man, Fargo thought with a little sting of regret.

The cantina was still there, flyblown as ever and surprisingly crowded. Also thankfully dim. Fargo picked the darkest corner and called for *pulque* and a local stew made from chicken and hot peppers.

The patrons were a mixture of Pueblo Indians and *mestizos,* and Fargo knew he stood out even in darkness. Especially to the prolonged stare of the one pure-blood Mexican in the place.

The big, burly, mustachioed man was wrapped in a

Saltillo blanket against the chill of the mountain night, and he had been watching Fargo since he came in.

Christ, Fargo thought, remembering. That same man had been feeding his face at the cantina in Chico Springs. And now that Fargo had a few days' beard stubble, the man was trying to place his face.

Fargo also noticed the old dragoon pistol suspended in a leather shoulder rig.

The man pushed away from the bar. Fargo, still shoveling in food, shifted onto his left hip to clear his draw. As the man neared, Fargo placed his spoon beside the plate and left his right hand free.

"Good evening, *señor,*" the man said with wary politeness, pausing well back from Fargo's table. *"Con permiso?"*

Fargo nodded and the man stepped closer. A big, solid, barrel-chested man now blocking Fargo's escape route.

"Perhaps we have seen each other before," he told Fargo, not making it a question.

Fargo drained his *pulque,* then shook his head. "Couldn't tell you. I ain't one to remember a face unless it's female."

"Pues . . . you look very familiar. Have you ever been to Chico Springs?"

"Few years ago."

A hardness seeped into the Mexican's eyes. "Perhaps . . . a few *days* ago?"

"Clean your ears or cut your hair, friend. I said I ain't been there lately. Anyhow, what if I was? No need taking the long way around the barn. State your charge or stand down—I like to eat in peace."

Fargo's determined gaze met the Mexican's suspicious one. The latter's hand slid a fractional inch toward his shoulder rig.

Fargo dropped a palm to the butt of his Colt. "You know the rules, *amigo.* Once a gun clears leather in a barroom, that's intent to kill."

For a long moment neither man moved. The cantina went as silent as a classroom after a hard question.

"My mistake, *señor,*" the Mexican finally said, turning away.

But Fargo didn't like something he'd seen in the man's eyes. Sure enough, after only three steps, quick as a striking snake, he filled his hand and whirled on Fargo.

Sensing the play, Fargo had already rolled out of his chair an eyeblink before the big slug blew the entire back out of it.

Fargo's Colt spat orange fire, and the slug drilled the Mexican through the heart. He was dead before he hit the floor.

Blue smoke curled from the revolver's muzzle. He gazed around the cantina.

"Unfortunately," he said politely, "a very rude man has disturbed our peace. I apologize for his bad manners. If I had enough money, I would pay for his burial."

"I saw everything, *señor*," volunteered a *mestizo* in the white cotton clothing of a peon. "It was self-defense, clearly. Carlos tried to kill you even after he was warned. He was a stupid man, *de veras*."

A murmur of assent moved through the crowd.

"We cannot bury him," another added. "He is a pagan who practices *hechicería,* witchcraft. We will feed him to the hogs."

Then, before anyone else could speak, a horrific female scream rent the fabric of the night.

"*Madre de Dios! Ayúdeme!* Please help me! *Fuego!*" Fire!

And that scream . . . so like the anguished cry Fargo had heard just three nights ago.

And then it all clicked into place, making his face go cold: that beautiful *mestiza* he'd passed, and the lingering sense of evil that marked the presence of Blaze Weston.

"Not *this* time, you son of a bitch," Fargo muttered as he raced from the cantina, the first man into the street. Back toward the far edge of the village, flames climbed high into the night sky, sawing crazily in the wind gusts.

Puddled adobe, with all that dried grass in it, burned faster than wood. He unlooped the Ovaro's reins, vaulted into the saddle, and thumped the stallion's ribs, racing toward the growing inferno.

The screams from inside the dwelling were bone-chilling. Several agitated neighbors were trying to get inside, but the heat drove them back.

Even before he reined in, Fargo had his blanket roll untied from the cantle straps. He leaped down, saturated the blanket with all the water in his gut bag, tossed it over himself and raced straight into the blistering heat of the flames encircling the front door.

Intense, searing heat licked at him, billows of acrid smoke choked him and made it damn near impossible to see. Then he glimpsed naked flesh.

Fargo had wondered why the young woman didn't try to escape the flames. Now he spotted her, through dense swirls of smoke, and realized why: She'd been tied up before Blaze torched the place. And judging from her swollen jaw, he'd knocked her out. Fortunately for her (or maybe with help from the crucifix over her bed), she'd come to in time to cry for help.

Her wooden bed frame was already on fire, the shuck mattress on the verge of exploding into flames. Fargo barely ducked to safety as part of the burning roof collapsed.

He threw the blanket over her, tossed her over his shoulder like a rolled carpet, then literally dived back out into the street as the entire structure collapsed in on itself.

The women quickly untied the hysterical, but unhurt, girl and hustled her off to the privacy of a nearby home. Fargo knew Blaze Weston couldn't be that far away yet— not as quickly as his signature fires did their dirty work.

And, unless Blaze returned north to Taos, Santa Cruz offered him only two trails out: south to Santa Fe or east to Chimayo. Either way, Weston's trail would be easy to locate. Fargo wanted to speak to the woman first. She might be able to tell him something, *anything,* about this enigmatic monster.

While some elderly and widowed village grandmothers calmed her down and clothed her, Fargo was treated to more liquor and food by the grateful males of the village.

"Rosalinda is her name," replied the cantina owner to Fargo's question.

"*Rosa linda*—pretty rose. She is that," he said. "Her man away?"

"Away with the angels, *en paz descansa*—may he rest in peace. Miguel was killed by raiding Comanches two years ago."

He paused, topped Fargo's glass, and added: "She has been with no man since then. Naturally, we men of the village find that a shame."

"Judging from what I saw of her," Fargo remarked, "I'd have to agree with you gents."

Rosalinda sent word she was ready to meet with her rescuer. They were given a candlelit room to themselves in a bare but neat adobe home.

Her modest home had been destroyed along with everything in it. Yet Fargo found her remarkably composed. Someone had given her a dark skirt and a white *camisola* baring beautiful shoulders.

She thanked him in rapid Spanish, one word tumbling out over another in her rush of emotions.

Fargo laughed and held up a hand. *"Mas despacio, querida!* Slow down, hon. Mostly I know border Spanish. That isn't quite the same as the pure Mex."

"You were so brave, *señor*."

"Call me Dave," Fargo said, wincing at the lie.

"Con gusto . . . Dave."

Damn, Fargo thought, looking at her in that light. It was incredible, the beauty that often resulted from the mix of Spanish and Indian blood.

Her bare shoulders were delicate—finely boned like her cheeks. The raven-black hair tumbled loose over them, and her lips seemed to glisten in the soft light.

"All right if I ask some questions?"

She nodded bravely.

"Did you get a good look at him?"

"No. I retire early, it was dark. He woke me up by placing a gun, I think, to my temple."

"Did he say anything?"

She nodded. Even in that subdued light, Fargo could see she was blushing.

"He said . . . strange things," she replied. "Over and over he called me a *puta*. He . . . he made me remove my shift. There was only some moonlight, but he seemed to see like a cat. He stared at me a long time."

Sure he sees like a cat, Fargo thought. *The crazy bastard must have permanent night vision by now.*

He cleared his throat for the delicate question. "Did he? . . ."

She shook her head, eyes fleeing suddenly from his. "I think . . . *pues,* I think he *wanted* to?"

"But you mean he . . . couldn't?"

She nodded. "His breathing—it was heavy, as if with lust. And his voice—*ay, Dios!* Like a whisper, only harsh. As he . . . as he rubbed himself, he began crying. He said it was my fault."

"*Your* fault?"

She cast her gaze downward.

"*Sí.* Because . . . because the devil was hiding in the place between my legs. He said he would 'purify' me."

A chill slid down Fargo's spine. Blaze Weston sounded like the craziest bastard he'd ever encountered—but crazy didn't mean stupid, as his amazing elusiveness proved.

"Then what?" he coaxed.

"He hit me with the gun. And when I woke up, I was trapped in my bed, on the verge of death. Until a very brave man was sent by God to save me."

"You have family here?"

She shook her head. A tear formed at the corner of one eye, and she swiped at it.

"I could *never* live here after this. First *mi marido,* my husband, was killed by Comanches. And now this. I could never feel safe here."

Fargo nodded. "Where will you go?"

"I have a married sister in Chimayo. It is very near this place, only a few miles east." She paused, then added: "Dave. Will *you* take me in the morning? Only with you would I ever feel safe. That . . . *diablo* is still out there somewhere."

Fargo remembered the news the freighter had told him earlier about Jimmy Davis in Springer.

"There's a telegraph office in Chimayo now, right?" he asked her.

Rosalinda nodded.

"Good. I'll take you to Chimayo in the morning and send an important telegram."

And just hope I'm not too late, Fargo thought. He hated to let Blaze Weston go, for now, but he had to try to help Bobbie Jean's brother.

His eyes met Rosalinda's in the candlelight. Two years since that beautiful young woman's had a man, Fargo reminded himself. And the way she was boldly meeting his eyes, she must have been thinking the same thing.

"You are going after this man?" she asked.

"Been after him for three days now. He killed a woman in Chico Springs and a man and wife in Springer."

"I can tell from your face, your manner, that you will stop him. You are a man who makes his strength and confidence felt immediately."

"I won't lie," Fargo admitted. "Where he's concerned, 'confident' I'm not."

The old *abuela* hustled in from the only other room. "You must sleep, Rosalinda," she fussed over the girl.

A smile split her seamed face when she turned to Fargo.

"And you, brave Señor Dave, will sleep here tonight. I will make a soft bed for you in this room. Come, Rosalinda, let's put you to bed."

"Good night, Dave," Rosalinda said in her musical voice, eyes lingering on his longingly.

Fargo went back outside, where the ashes of Rosalinda's home still smoldered. He circled the place several times, studying the ground in the moonlight.

And then he spotted, in the confused pattern of prints, the familiar, hobnail boot prints.

Just looking at them turned his stomach. Blaze Weston had chosen the trail to Chimayo.

Fargo returned to his room, where a soft pallet awaited him on the rammed-earth floor. The old woman had also left a pan of water, a lump of yucca-root soap, and a towel.

Fargo stripped, cleaned up, and forced himself to shave again—his thick, heavy beard had grown back quickly, as if resentful of the change after so many years. Then, all three of his weapons to hand, he crawled into his pallet. Not as plush as the Dorsey, but better than a cold camp on rocky ground.

Rosa linda—pretty rose.

Fargo was weary, and already his eyes felt weighted with coins. He saw her honey skin, the full, glistening lips, the woman's hunger as she'd gazed at him. . . .

Outside, an owl hooted. As he drifted down a long tunnel into sleep, Fargo heard the reassuring champing sound as the Ovaro took the grass off the slope behind the house.

A door meowed open, and Fargo snapped awake, filling his hand with blue steel.

"Dave? *Con permiso?*"

A smile tugged at his lips. Even when she whispered, Rosalinda's musical voice was unmistakable.

"Permission granted," he assured her moonlit form as she crossed to his pallet. She held a blanket snugged around her.

"Maria made a point of telling me she is a heavy sleeper. That is not so true. She *wanted* me to come to you."

"Then that makes two of us," Fargo said.

"Three," she assured him.

She knelt at the edge of the pallet, holding the blanket closed in front of her.

"You saw me naked earlier," she whispered, so close to his ear her breath was warm, moist, and tickling. "But you did not *see* me naked. I want you to."

Rosalinda dropped the blanket, and Fargo felt heat pulse in his groin. A silver-white shaft of moonlight, slanting in through the unshuttered window, showed Fargo a sylvan nymph right out of erotic mythology.

"*Te gustas?* Do you like what you see?"

Fargo's woman-hungry eyes took in pointy, perfectly sculpted breasts, wide, flaring hips, an excitingly thick and dark bush.

"*Me gusta mucho,*" he assured her, cupping a breast and taking the nipple into his mouth.

Her need was so intense that a shudder moved through her as he teased her nipple into a hard little bullet.

"*La otra?*" she begged, and he obligingly gave the same treatment to her other breast.

In mere moments she was hotter than a branding iron, her soft gasps starting to turn into urgent panting.

Fargo was fully aroused now. He threw back the blanket, and Rosalinda stared at his straining, curving length.

"I did not realize a man could be so *big* down there," she confessed, gripping his shaft at the base and giving him a squeeze.

Pleasure jolted through Fargo's groin as she stroked his length.

"It's never been *too* big yet," he assured her. "Here, let me show you."

Fargo parted her satiny thighs and she hitched one leg over, mounting him. Fargo bent his shaft to the perfect angle. Rosalinda was glazed and slick with her desire, and he slid in as neatly as a dagger into a sheath.

"Now *that* ain't too big, is it?" he whispered on a moan of pleasure.

"*Ay, caramba!*" she exclaimed in a throaty whisper. "Oh, not too big, no. It feels so . . . oh, never, *never* like this!"

Her pent-up need was now unleashed as from a floodgate. Harder, faster, more intensely she thrust up and down Fargo's length.

"*Ay, Dios!*" she cried out, starting to thrash around with wild abandon as climax after climax exploded through her.

Fargo, his own eruption only seconds away, was now literally lifting her off the pallet as he drove deep to the core of her need, spending himself in a shuddering abandon of pleasure.

So intense was their coupling that, for uncounted minutes, they lay in a dazed tangle of entwined arms and legs.

"I must be shameless," she finally broke the silence in a whisper, licking his curls of chest hair. "I want it all over again."

Fargo guided her hand to his manhood, which stood at rigid attention.

"Never be afraid to ask for seconds," he assured her, rolling her over and climbing into his favorite saddle.

9

After a simple breakfast of cornmeal mush, the old woman, Maria, presented Rosalinda with a breechloader and a doeskin ammo pouch.

"My husband," Maria said, making the sign of the cross, "was the ferry operator at Rio Mora for many years. Despite the law forbidding us to own weapons, he kept this with him. Take it, Rosalinda, and always keep it by your bed."

Fargo glanced at the weapon. It was a cap-and-ball single-shot rifle made by William W. Marston of New York City. A Marston rifle always had an excellent ramp sight on it, making it an accurate piece.

Rosalinda looked at the weapon doubtfully.

"I know nothing of its use," she confessed.

"Easier than rolling off a log," Fargo assured her. "Just always be careful handling it, and if trouble comes, don't even pick it up if you aren't dead set on using it. Never bluff with a firearm."

Quickly he showed her how to charge and fire the old breechloader.

"Just chew open the cardboard cartridge," he said, spitting out a wad of brown paper, "and thumb the ball through the loading gate, right there. Then you just poke the rest of the cartridge in, like so, close the breech, and your primer's built into that leather base on the cartridge."

He thumbed the hammer to full cock. "That's all you do to get it ready to fire."

He thumbed it back off cock. "I'll lash it to my horse

until we get to your sister's place in Chimayo. That way you'll be legal."

When Fargo and Rosalinda went outside, a slat-ribbed gelding waited in front of the hut, already saddled. A group of well-wishers stood waiting to say good-bye to Rosalinda.

"This was once a plow horse, for its sins," apologized an old peon wearing a straw hat and rope sandals. "But it is broken to the saddle. Rosalinda can leave the old nag with my brother Pablo in Chimayo."

Fargo glanced at the cinch and grinned. Whoever had tightened the girth had been duped by the old nag's cunning. He undid the cinch and tugged it tight and quick. Otherwise, the crafty animal would sneak a big breath and toss the rider later from a loose saddle.

"That man from last night," Rosalinda said with a shudder as they rode out. "I know you went out later to find his trail. Did you?"

Fargo nodded, not wanting to lie about it. She had a right to know.

"At the moment, he's headed right toward Chimayo."

"All the saints," she murmured, coffee brown eyes widened in fright.

"You want to stay in Santa Cruz instead?" Fargo offered.

"But . . . *you* are going to Chimayo?"

He nodded.

"Then so am I. I only feel safe with you."

Chimayo lay only about three hours' ride to the east, an ancient village almost forty miles north of Santa Fe. It was an important site to many Christianized locals, because it was home to El Santuario—one more of many unpretentious little chapels throughout New Mexico.

But the trail was a dangerous stretch that had Fargo worried. At times it was high elevation, with rock parapets, which meant possible trouble. There were also plenty of thickets, cutbanks, and other good ambush points.

And high above the trail, on the rimrock, the Apaches were watching.

"She will sell high to some rich man with a hacienda in the south country," Jemez Gray Eyes said. "I know

90

that one. Comanches sent her man under. She will sell high."

The night before, Jemez and his hard-bitten band of Mescaleros and Jicarillas had made camp in the lee of a long spine of rimrock. The crosswinds were fierce here, and colder than in the lower elevations. They buffeted the men from every direction. But they always felt safer in the high places.

The Fighting-Men, as was their ancient custom, had slept behind low windbreaks made of stones.

"And *this* beauty," chimed in Hoyero, "will not be traded for guns or horses. We will take only the glittering metal disks."

Although not as rapidly as the Navajos had, Apaches, too, were starting to realize that gold and silver coins had great value to all the invaders of their historic homeland.

"All this land, as far as you can see," Jemez said, making a sweeping gesture with one arm, "was once called Apacheria by our enemies, who stayed out. Then Coronado came and called it New Spain. Next it was called Mejico, and the brown ones placed a bounty on our scalps."

Jemez paused, his black agate eyes studying the pair below on the trail.

"Now these white-skins like him call our land America. It is still Apacheria to we who are the Fighting-Men. But that one?"

He pointed down toward the man on the handsome pinto stallion.

"This Son of Light . . . he is widely respected for his fighting skills. Let us put him to the test. Mahko!"

One of Jemez's fellow Mescaleros stepped forward.

"You are a good shot," Jemez told him. "Get below and send them a greeting from the Fighting-Men."

Fargo realized it long before Rosalinda did.

The Apaches had begun one of their favorite harassing tactics: "showing" themselves, a little game they played to unnerve a man and test his mettle.

It began with brief glimpses. Fargo would glance up and sight one standing openly on a ledge. As they advanced along the winding trail, the braves began to appear lower and lower down.

"Madre de Dios!" Rosalinda gasped behind him, and Fargo realized she'd finally spotted one of them. "Dave! I saw—"

"Just stay calm," he cut in without turning around to look at her. "Don't let them see you're scared."

The next brave Fargo spotted was flashing a knife. Upping the ante.

"Will they attack us?" Rosalinda asked, her voice tight with fear.

"Like most Indians, they're notional. We'll have to wait and see."

You just can't tell, Fargo thought, *with a bunch like that—probably an outlaw band cast from their clans.* Theirs was the primitive, nomadic lot of a people who had been driven to the harshest, hottest, driest, most dangerous places in the Southwest—some places so remote they were not yet on maps.

As the twig is bent, Fargo mused, his eyes going distant for a moment. Right now, he knew exactly how they felt. Hounded, unsafe day or night, always waiting for the next hidden rifle to speak its piece.

"Ojo!" Rosalinda cried. "Look out! That one is pointing a rifle at us!"

"Steady, girl," Fargo said. "They're testing us."

"Why are they doing this?" she asked plaintively.

Because they want you, sweet and juicy little beauty, Fargo thought. *And that bunch won't have any trouble of the kind Blaze Weston had last night, when his manhood failed to perform. After they've had their use of you, they'll sell you into slavery.*

"They do it because we're here," Fargo replied. "Some shots are coming, but *don't* panic."

Despite the warning, Rosalinda cried out when a bullet kicked up a geyser of dirt in front of the Ovaro.

The bullet-savvy stallion flinched, but kept moving.

"Steady, *querida*," Fargo called to Rosalinda. "We're just riding off to a Sunday picnic, that's all."

Another plume of dust spat up when a bullet splatted into the trail, this one closer.

Fargo used his knees and a familiar, soothing tone to

calm the Ovaro. It was more of a job, however, to get Rosalinda's stove-in nag under control.

"Dave," Rosalinda pleaded. "They are going to shoot us!"

"They'd've done it by now," he assured her. "Right now it's a game."

The next shot hornet-buzzed past Fargo's left ear.

"Ain't had this much fun since the hogs ate Maw-Maw!" Fargo called out cheerfully to the scowling Apache, who now stood only thirty yards away on a basalt ledge.

Now the "game" had to end, Fargo told himself, and he had to end it. Of all the tribes he'd had set-tos with, none surpassed the Apaches in ferocity, courage, and cunning. The key, when confronting them, was to mingle respect with strength.

And since they could be unbelievably cruel to an enemy, it was best not to become one.

Again the Apache raised his carbine, preparing to fire.

With a blur of speed, Fargo's Colt cleared leather, then leaped into his fist.

The Apache loosed a bray of pain, his dropped carbine clattering among the rocks. He held up his left hand, the one he'd used to steady the barrel, and stared at it in astonishment.

The tip of his left index finger had been precisely blown off at the first joint.

Evidently Fargo must have passed his test with the Apaches. He and Rosalinda made the rest of the ride unmolested.

"There's Chimayo," Fargo said as they rounded the shoulder of a mountain.

The village was a tight cluster of adobe buildings down below in a fertile valley. Wild columbine colored the surrounding pastures and meadows with splashes of sky blue. Workers filled the *milpas,* or communal fields.

"You still see his tracks, don't you?" Rosalinda asked, watching Fargo study the trail as they descended the final slope into Chimayo.

He nodded, saying nothing. But Fargo feared there was going to be a hot time in the old town tonight, unless he could flush Blaze Weston out first.

They reached the outskirts of the village. In these remote mountain settlements, Christian and Indian religions often mixed. White crosses alternated with prayer plumes planted to curry favor with the gods.

"May we stop here a moment?" Rosalinda asked. "I wish to give thanks for our safe journey."

"Here" was El Santuario de Chimayo, a small chapel nestled among cottonwoods.

"Take your time. I'll wait out here."

"Please come inside with me?"

"Well . . . no offense, pretty lady, but me and churches aren't exactly too well acquainted. I'm not precisely what you'd call a 'believer.'"

"Everyone is welcome at El Santuario."

Fargo was about to beg off. Just then, however, he realized something: the tracks of Blaze Weston's horse—turned in at the lane leading to the chapel.

True, another set proved Blaze had already left again. But suddenly Fargo wanted to see what might have interested him so much.

"Sure, let's have a gander at this place with the miracle dirt."

She smiled. "So you do know about it? Well, the miracle dirt is there. *Ven conmigo.* Come with me, I'll show you."

Fargo threw off, helped Rosalinda down, then walked her under the rustling cottonwoods toward the open front door.

Fargo glanced down at the sand path, his stomach going queasy with loathing when he recognized Weston's boot prints.

"Don't be afraid," Rosalinda teased him, misunderstanding his sudden apprehension. She tugged him through the doors. "If sinners are struck by lightning, we'll both be hit—after last night," she added, flushing.

"These doors left unlocked all the time?" Fargo asked, glancing around at the cool, dim interior.

"*Claro.* This is God's house and a sanctuary."

Maybe so, thought Fargo, *and it looks like the devil's been poking around lately, too.*

The interior was sparse and simple, with a puncheon floor and raw-lumber pews. Niches in the thick old walls held plaster statues of the saints. Despite the overall simplicity of El Santuario, however, the elaborate altar featured intricate bas-relief designs in hammered gold and silver.

Several black-robed nuns knelt at the altar, fingering their rosaries.

"Look," Rosalinda said, pointing to one wall of the anteroom where she and Fargo stood. It was covered with rows of crutches. "Those belonged to people who came here lame and left healed."

"With all those crutches," Fargo remarked mildly, "wouldn't you expect to see at least one wooden leg?"

Rosalinda playfully hit his arm. *"Bárbaro!"*

She pointed to a small, candlelit room to the left of the altar.

"Exactly in the center of that room," she said, "is the hole with the sacred soil. The holy dirt from that ground has been taken out by believers for many, many years. Yet, miraculously, it is always replaced."

"Uh-huh," Fargo said politely, more interested right now in those hobnailed boot prints than in lore.

Rosalinda prayed at the altar while Fargo tracked the sandy prints. Blaze seemed to have made one quick pass around the chapel—and Fargo doubted it was for religious inspiration. This place would not ignite easily from outside—this was not grass-impregnated adobe, but solid baked mud.

But the inside . . . that was all wood. Old, weather-sapped wood that made for perfect tinder.

"C'mon," he said, the moment Rosalinda finished praying. "Let's get you to your sister's, then I got a telegram to send."

Rosalinda's sister, Serafina, lived just past the southern edge of the village. A handsome woman perhaps five years older than Rosalinda, she was weeding a strip of side garden as the two rode up.

The sisters greeted each other effusively in rapid Spanish mixed with an *indio* dialect Fargo didn't recognize.

"And what's your friend's name?" Serafina asked shyly.

Fargo had noticed how Indians in New Mexico considered it bad manners to ask a person his name directly, such was the important power of a name. It was the custom to ask a friend instead.

"Dave Tutt," Rosalinda replied, and Fargo again felt like a weasel.

"Will you have *comida* with us?" Serafina asked. "There is plenty."

"Con gusto," Fargo replied. "But first I need to send a telegram."

"What in blue blazes?"

Major Jeff Carlson, commanding officer of the garrison at Fort Union, had just been handed an odd message from the post telegrapher:

> SEND TROOPS TO SPRINGER IMMEDIATELY
> STOP CITIZENS COMMITTEE ABOUT TO
> EXECUTE INNOCENT PRISONER IN ABSENCE
> OF SHERIFF STOP WILL EXPLAIN ALL LATER
> MISTER BRASS BUTTONS

A slow grin spread under the major's neat line of mustache.

Only one man had the audacity to call him Mr. Brass Buttons.

"Skye Fargo," he said aloud. "So you're still among the living, old friend?"

Not for one second had Carlson ever believed the wild tales about Skye Fargo, arsonist and woman-killer. The major had known and worked with Fargo—as friend, scout, hunter—since the days when Carlson was a shavetail fresh out of West Point. And he'd never met a better man, in or out of uniform.

"Wexley!" he called out to his orderly.

A young second lieutenant appeared in the doorway. "Sir?"

"Tell Sergeant Avery to pick ten men immediately. They're to be issued short rations and forty rounds of ammunition apiece. I want them dispatched immediately to Springer, where they will seize the town jail under martial law and take custody of any prisoners until Sheriff Rafferty returns. Any 'vigilantes' who attempt to interfere will be arrested—or shot, if need be."

"Yes, sir! Right away, sir!"

When Wexley had left, Carlson gazed at the telegram again, more thoughtfully this time. He knew damn well why Skye had not shown up to begin his new duty as a scout for a road-building crew. He had his name to clear and one hell of a monster to stop.

"Good luck, old friend," he said softly.

10

After a hearty meal provided by Serafina, Fargo went out into the sneeze-bright sunshine of midday. *Weston doesn't seem to strike by day,* Fargo reminded himself. *Not with his fires, anyway.* Probably because the darkness, besides hiding him, literally magnified the "glory" of his achievement.

Skye Fargo had never claimed he could read sign on a sick mind. But common sense and the clues were clear. Weston was unable to rape the beautiful woman he desired. So he torched them to death in the same beds where he'd failed to master them.

And the other fires that didn't involve young women? That was just Weston "playing with himself" until the great, climactic fires gave him ultimate release.

Fargo walked down to the chapel, checked it thoroughly inside and out, then strolled around the entire village, drawing plenty of curious glances.

No sign of Blaze Weston. *But he's here,* Fargo told himself. *As sure as sunrise in the morning. In the area if not the village.*

The Ovaro had been turned out into a little paddock behind the house of his hosts. Fargo used a hoof pick and began removing a few tiny pebbles embedded in the stallion's hooves.

Normally Fargo tried to do this once a day. But he hadn't had time lately to do so. However, ignoring the pebbles any longer could cause a crack to develop up into the fetlock, making his horse founder at a critical moment.

Pebbles scuffed behind him and Fargo whirled, slapping leather.

"Dave?"

Rosalinda had come outside to find him. She was freshly bathed and now looked pretty in one of her sister's blue skirts with a white *camisola* that bared both beautiful shoulders.

"Are you going to shoot me?" she teased him.

"Jesus, girl, I damn near cleared the holster. Don't sneak up on a fella like that. Especially these days."

"I saw your face when Otero talked about the strange behavior of the animals this morning. He *is* here, isn't he? The same man who tried to kill me last night?"

Fargo nodded.

"Been here, and my guess is he's coming back," he replied. "Right now I'd bet a king's ransom he's holed up outside of Chimayo. Holed up tighter than a rabbit in a hollow log. Waiting until twilight."

"You are tending to your horse. Does this mean you are riding out now to find him?"

Fear had crept into her tone, and Fargo knew why. After what she'd been through last night, a fellow she called Dave Tutt was her only reliable protector.

"Don't you worry," he assured her. "Mostly I'll be keeping an eye on you, which is no awful job. And now and then I'll take a quick stroll around the village."

Relief flooded her pretty face.

"He'd *like* me to come flush him out," Fargo added. "That way he can kill me and have a free hand. So I don't figure to accommodate him in his plans."

She flashed him a smile full of pearly teeth. "I have faith in your brain and courage. But he is a monster beyond words to describe him. *Ten cuidado?*"

"Yes, I'll be careful," he replied. "There's no other way to be, with him."

She had something else to say, something that made her cast her eyes demurely downward.

"Dave?"

"Hmm?"

"Earlier today, when I prayed at El Santuario?"

"Yeah?"

"I only gave thanks for my rescue last night and our safe journey past the Apaches. I did not ask forgiveness for . . . for what we did last night."

Fargo grinned. "Guess what? I don't plan on asking for any forgiveness, either."

"Of course, you are a pagan. And a good pagan is better than a bad Catholic. I cannot lie, in a prayer, and say I am sorry when I am not. Especially . . ."

She flushed. "Especially since I will be leaving the shutters on my bedroom window unlocked tonight—in case you should choose to come to me."

The sudden explosion of heat in Fargo's groin answered *that* invitation. He remembered her last night, opening the blanket to show herself to him. And later, thrusting up and down on top of him, riding his length to climax after climax . . .

"You do that," he told her. "But under one condition."

"Cuál?"

"Keep that rifle Maria gave you right beside the bed."

"Lo juro. I swear it."

"Good. And since I plan on knocking on those shutters later, you just make damn sure you know who you're shooting."

At the halfway point, on the trail leading from Chimayo to the nearby Nambe Pueblo, stood a tumble of rocks larger than a two-story house.

Old Indian legends claimed the Great Thunderbird had dropped those rocks there to kill a *bruja,* a witch. Perhaps so, for Blaze Weston had circled around behind the rocks and found a spot where he and his horse could wedge themselves in and hide.

Before he did, however, he wiped out his tracks and continued along the path, leaving a false trail to the east. Finally, he doubled back through the trees to his new hiding place.

He would sleep, eat a few crusts of ash-pone, then move on again.

This Fargo was a worthy opponent. But without question Blaze would return to Chimayo, Fargo be damned. He must, after what he had seen earlier today.

This morning, as he passed El Santuario, he had seen a painted harlot go into the chapel. And the priest out front had smiled and greeted her as she did so! Letting that soiled dove bring the devil in with her.

And that pretty little whore last night in Santa Cruz—Fargo had "saved" her from her own purification by flames. But he wouldn't save that bunch of sluts at the Queen of Sheba in Springer. Blaze would make sure of that by killing Fargo first.

Hell, boy. You got a tallywhacker that don't whack.

Again the white-hot, liquid rage filled him.

"Hellfire's coming," he promised as he lay his head on his saddle for a thirty-minute sleep. "Oh, hellfire's coming!"

Just after sunset, Fargo stood in the small anteroom of El Santuario, closely studying the interior of the chapel.

Besides the dozens of votive candles, *farolitos* burned along the side walls. A handful of the local faithful were seated among the pews, praying or saying their beads. A monk in a roped tunic knelt before the altar, head bowed deep in prayer.

Fargo went out into the grainy twilight. He had purposely left the Ovaro in the paddock on the opposite end of town and walked here.

Sticking to the apron of shadows close to the chapel, Fargo slowly and carefully made his way along all four sides, Colt to hand.

He paused at sight of the *camposanto* out back, where rows of crosses and stones represented generations. The wind came shrieking in off the Sangre de Cristo slopes, chilling him. Somewhere, a coyote yipped mournfully, and Fargo heard it as a potential death omen.

He spotted no sign of Blaze Weston. But then again, the man could almost literally disappear without a trace when he wanted to.

A farmer's cart rattled past out front. Somewhere a dog barked, setting off a chain reaction throughout the village. When the racket died down, the wind rose in howling, whipping gusts.

It was night, Fargo reminded himself, and the Weeping Woman was now wandering all over the region, her grief in the sound of the wind. Better she than others who stalked the night.

Fargo poked his head back inside the chapel. The worshippers in the pews had dwindled to two. The monk was still deep in prayer.

All secure inside. But something felt wrong to Fargo—his "goose tickle" was back, that familiar tingle in his scalp that meant trouble was a cat whisker away.

A shadowy form approached on foot along the village street, taking no pains to sneak or hide. Fargo watched it take pleasing shape as Rosalinda.

"Serafina sends this," she said, handing him a pottery mug of steaming coffee.

"Serafina's an angel, and tell her I said so."

"I will not. She has an eye for you, I can tell. And *you*, Dave Tutt, have an eye for the women."

"Bless them all in several languages," Fargo admitted.

He sipped from the cup, then added: "But I thought we agreed you were staying home with Serafina and Otero—and the gun," he added with emphasis.

"We did, and I am sorry. But . . . it is just . . . thinking about last night, how it felt to once again . . ."

She trailed off, but Fargo could hear the quickening of her breath as passion got her in its grip.

"You quiet little firecracker," Fargo teased her. "Admit it, *chica*. You're hot for more of it, are'n'cha?"

She nodded, too embarrassed to speak.

Fargo laughed. "Well, hell, so am I. Should we do it in *front* of the chapel or behind?"

She slapped his arm. "I only meant . . . I mean . . . I will be naked in my bed, waiting. Now I will go."

"Hold it, cottontail."

She had started to hurry away, but Fargo caught her by the arm. "Now that you've broken the rules, best to let me escort you home. Hang on a minute."

To be absolutely certain, Fargo glanced inside the chapel again. All was well. He also took another quick turn around the exterior of El Santuario.

"Let's hurry," he told Rosalinda, linking his arm through hers.

It took about ten minutes to walk her home. On the way back, still about fifty yards from the chapel, Fargo glimpsed something glittering in the shallow ditch beside the path.

He knelt down to investigate: It was a fancy rosary, with colored glass beads that reflected the moonlight.

And there, a few feet away, Fargo spotted the hand that had been holding it—and the rest of the nearly naked man who lay stone dead in the ditch, his head swimming in his own blood.

His throat had been slashed ear to ear—exactly like the killing of the old hostler in Chico Springs.

A rosary . . . a nearly naked man killed in the obvious style of Blaze Weston. . . . Why nearly naked?

Unless. . . .

"Shit!" Fargo swore out loud, drawing steel and bolting toward the chapel. "That damned 'monk!'"

Fargo burst through the anteroom of the chapel. The place reeked of coal oil. The worshippers were either gone or dead by now.

And the "monk"—votive candle in hand—now stood over the cloth-draped altar.

Fargo could see the altar's covering—it was soaked!

Blaze spun around when Fargo cried out his name, his big cap-and-ball aimed at Fargo's lights.

The Trailsman veered to one side, the big pistol exploded with a cannon roar in the chapel, and then Fargo's heart turned to ice as Blaze dropped the candle on the altar.

With a horrific *whoosh,* the cloth covering erupted in flames. Weston, lumbering like a buffalo but incredibly fast, bolted toward the little door behind the altar, and now Fargo finally sprayed lead at him.

Again and again the Colt leaped in his fist, filling the chapel with the acrid stink of spent powder. Still on the run, he leathered his gun and jerked the Arkansas Toothpick from its boot sheath. But Blaze had slipped through the door and was gone.

Fargo put out the flaming altar with water from a nearby ewer. In the brief time he'd been walking Rosalinda home and returning, Blaze had managed to rig the entire interior for an inferno. Coal-oil soaked tinder, Fargo noticed, was strategically placed so that one quick pass with a lit candle would have gutted the chapel.

And now, Blaze was still out there. And if Fargo started right now, he'd have a fresh trail. As much as he regretted passing on that invitation from Rosalinda, salting this killer's tail came first.

11

Skye Fargo hated night riding, and tried to avoid it like he would a temperance lecture. There were too many rocks, gopher holes, and other dangers that could bring a horse up seriously lame. And in Fargo's present mess, he'd be dead without the Ovaro.

But a man couldn't avoid everything he hated doing. And Blaze Weston was so damned dangerous and destructive that Fargo had to break the usual rules. He had to stay on that sick bastard like ugly on a buzzard even if it meant riding in darkness black as new tar. As the incident tonight in Chimayo proved, constant pressure was the only defense against Blaze.

And even that was no guarantee.

By the time Fargo passed the still and silent Nambe Pueblo, he had a good idea which way Weston was headed: either southwest, toward Santa Fe, or due south toward Pecos.

Weston took no pains to hide his trail. He was moving quickly, and so far he'd played no more of his sick little games. He seemed bent on putting as much distance as he could between himself and Fargo.

But for what purpose? Fargo didn't believe Weston was "fleeing." He had no more fear in him than a rifle did—he was too crazy. Much more likely, he just wanted time to set up an ambush.

Ambush . . . that could come at any time on these narrow, closely grown mountain trails.

Fargo had his Henry out of its boot, holding it with the butt-plate resting on his right thigh. Luminous moonlight washed the landscape in ghostly blue, and the sound of the Ovaro's hoof clops seemed dangerously magnified.

"Up against it again, old warhorse," he muttered. "We *do* get all the fool's errands, don't we?"

But his faithful stallion had no complaint. And every time Fargo recalled the dying scream of poor Elena Vargas, he knew this was no fool's errand.

"This is turning into grand sport," Jemez Gray Eyes remarked with obvious satisfaction. "The spectacle pleases me greatly. Two white-skins, each determined to kill the other first. I am for wagering on this."

He and his small band were in the high rock parapets of the very spine of the Sangre de Cristo range. Following ancient traces known only to the Apaches, they were able to keep an eagle's eye on the rider below them, this Son of Light who rode the fine pinto stallion.

"My wager is on the evil one," said Llanero, a Jicarilla from the "Plains people" branch of his Apache group. "The hair-face on the sorrel. His is cunning and ruthless. Never have I seen such evil. He has dark power behind him—the power of those who live by night."

"You speak words a man can pick up and hold," agreed Mahko, a Mescalero. "But Son of Light has medicine, too. More—he has *this*."

Mahko held his left hand up in the moonlight, showing them how the tip was missing from the first finger.

"A true Fighting-Man did this to me," he said proudly. "And yet . . . he respected me. This finger is nothing to me. He did not injure my shooting finger."

This was indeed impressive character, and the rest were silent for some time. They had witnessed the event, after all.

It was Jemez's favorite, Hoyero, who broke the silence.

"Whichever of them wins," he said, "is of no importance to me. I only know that fine stallion will be on my string."

"Hoyero is right. *Let* them kill each other for our sport," Jemez repeated. "We will take horses, weapons, everything."

He held his stolen Mexican army carbine high into the air.

"Now we, too, have the sticks that speak with the voice of the thunderbird. So they turn on each other? Good. Fewer bullets we need to waste."

By the time the sun broke over the serrated peaks of the surrounding mountains, Fargo knew where Blaze was headed: straight toward Pecos.

Fargo was following the Old Pecos Trail now, fresh on Blaze's track. The Trailsman, saddle-weary, reined in to let the Ovaro blow. Fargo breathed in deeply the clean, nose-tickling tang of green alfalfa fields.

The Pecos river valley lay spread out below him, a lush, green ribbon meandering through the parched brown hills surrounding it.

Rocky bluffs rose on both sides of the trail. Fargo studied them while he rested, trying to figure Weston's game.

Is he really going to Pecos, to jump me there? Fargo wondered. *Or does he lay down a trail, backtrack, and then dry-gulch me?*

Fargo pushed on toward the valley. He passed a few *indios,* some wearing their silver and turquoise jewelry, even though they were headed into the fields.

He asked them, in Spanish and English, if they'd seen a bearded Anglo rider pass by recently. They merely shook their heads, either not understanding or not wanting to get involved. Fargo suspected the latter and couldn't blame them. Outsiders had brought nothing but trouble and disease and death to these people.

He got more fortunate with his next encounter: a grizzled old prospector riding the ugliest mountain mustang Fargo had ever seen.

The old man laughed when he saw Fargo staring at his horse. It was barely thirteen hands, and the old man's scuffed boots were dragging on the ground.

"It's true this damned ugly broom-tail has bony withers," he greeted Fargo, spitting an amber streamer beside the trail. "But he's got good bottom and always bucks to the same pattern."

"Praise the tall, but ride the small," Fargo quoted the old Spanish saying.

"Now iffen I had me a horse like *that*," the prospector added, nodding toward the Ovaro, "I'd sell him in Santa Fe and quit scratching for color in these goldang mountains. Hell, I'll get pussy from the Queen of England 'fore I ever strike a lode."

"Passed any riders this morning?" Fargo asked him. "Specifically, a bearded hombre, prob'ly wearing buckskins?"

"Ridin' a sorrel?"

"That I don't know."

The old-timer spat again. "Le'me see, now. This feller I seen was wearin' a buckskin shirt. And he was headed toward the ruins at Pecos. Leastways, I call it ruins. Outside of a few Indian stragglers still hanging on, it ain't really a settlement no more. Matter fact, it's a damn good place to ride wide of. Snakes been showing up there lately, and they ain't the kind that hatch from eggs."

"I've heard that," Fargo conceded.

"I only seen him from afar," the old salt added. "But I'll tell you flat out, young fella, something about just *lookin'* at him gave me the fantods. Iffen you're after him, take some advice: Just leave it alone."

"Can't, dad. This one's a killer."

"It's *full* of killers in Pecos, boy. No man rides in there and comes out alive unless he's one of 'em. Luck to you, son. You'll be needing it, for a surety."

It was late in the morning, and Bobbie Jean Davis was busy laying out Cynthia Robinson's afternoon outfit when Butch Robinson returned to the house.

"If you want to visit your brother like you been whining," he told her, his eyes raking over her hungrily, "the Vigilance Committee says it's okay. But you'll have to come right now."

"Of course I want to see him!" she exclaimed, quickly untying her crisp white apron. "Vigilance Committee, my butt! You had no right to arrest him, nor to keep me from visiting him."

"Hell we didn't. We're the law while Rafferty's gone."

"The law? Don't make me sick. You and your father are the biggest damn criminals in this town!"

His lean mouth curled into a threatening sneer. "Now that's a stain upon the honor of my family name. You got some plans to back up that claim?"

"No, because I know you'll kill me."

"Now you're whistling. And before I kill you, I'm damned if I'm gonna waste what you got."

Bobbie Jean hurried past him, deftly avoiding his hand when he tried, as usual, to grab her bottom. *Oh, if only Skye Fargo was around to cut this two-bit bully down to size.*

She hurried to the jailhouse, Butch barely keeping up with her. The man called Josh was serving as "jailer" when she arrived. But why, she wondered, was Nate Robinson here? She thought he was at his brickyard.

She gasped when she spotted her brother, who was slumped against the wall of his cell. There was hardly a spot on his face that wasn't bruised or bloody.

"Jimmy!" she cried. But her brother had been so badly beaten that he hardly registered her presence.

She whirled angrily on the three men.

"You filthy *animals*! What did you do to him?"

Josh looked embarrassed and uncomfortable and couldn't meet her eye. But Butch just shrugged, his usual mocking grin in place.

Bobbie Jean had noticed how he'd been especially swaggering it around ever since Skye Fargo broke his nose—no doubt, he was doing so to compensate for his shame at the bulbous lump of plaster cast covering it.

"Stupid bastard resisted arrest," Butch replied. "If you want to talk to him, shut your squawk box and get in there."

Butch grabbed the key ring off the desk and unlocked the door, letting her inside the cell. But she had barely even gotten a few words out before Butch announced, "That's it, sugar butt. Visiting hours are now over."

She gaped in pure astonishment at him. "Over? But you just said—"

He had opened the cell door and now pulled her roughly outside, wrenching her shoulder.

"I've had my belly full of your sass," he informed her.

Again she shuddered as his eyes raked over her, raw with mean, filthy lust. "And pretty soon *your* belly is gonna be full of me, if you take my drift. Now get the hell outta here before I slap the shit outta you."

"Now, now, Butchie boy," Nate soothed in his oily manner. "No need to be unpleasant about this. See you at the house, Bobbie Jean."

Even as Butch pushed her toward the door, her limbs went heavy with dread.

"Nate?" she demanded. "What's going on here?"

"Shoo along, Roberta, shoo along," he told her. "This is men's business."

She whirled again on Butch, fists balled on her shapely hips. Anger had turned her polished-apple cheeks even brighter.

"You *won't* get away with whatever you've got planned," she warned him. "None of you will."

"That right?"

His right thumb stroked the walnut grip on his Remington. "And you tell me, missy. Just *who* is gonna stop us?"

"That answer's as plain as the end of your broken nose," she shot back. "Literally."

Butch's lean, hard face was suddenly etched in acid.

"Your goddamn *hero*, huh? It don't take no guts to cold-cock a man and then run like a river when the snow melts."

"That's not a man who 'runs' from anything."

"Yeah? Well, Pete Helzer, Dave Tutt, Skye Fargo—his name is *dead* next time I see him."

She reached for the door, her hand trembling. "Oh, you'll be seeing him, all right."

Something in her tone caused an uncertain glint in his eyes.

"The hell's that s'posed to mean?" he demanded, his voice a bit edgy.

"Do you really think," she asked, opening the door, "that you can call a man like Skye Fargo 'trash' and a 'coward' to his face and there won't be a reckoning? You remember that, too, before you lay another hand on my brother!"

She slammed the door shut so hard that the WANTED posters on the wall rattled.

"She's all mouth," Nate dismissed her. "Well, gents, we now have witnesses who'll say that Bobbie Jean came here today to see her brother. And guess what?"

He reached past Josh and opened the top drawer of the desk. He removed a slim dagger in a leather sheath.

"She must have sneaked this in to him," Nate continued, "knowing he was guilty as sin for the fires he's started, and for the ones he paid Fargo to start. Naturally Jimmy would do *anything* to escape."

Nate put the knife on the floor and kicked it under the bars. It slid inside the cell. Jimmy stared at it, still not comprehending.

"And then," Butch took over the carefully rehearsed story, "poor Josh here was overpowered while trying to take him his lunch."

"Boys," Josh said uncertainly, "I don't like this. Jimmy—"

"Need I remind you, Josh," Nate interjected smoothly, "about a warrant out for your arrest in Texas? Something about a fourteen-year-old girl?"

Josh, looking glum and defeated, shut up.

"All right," Butch resumed the story. "Jimmy got the keys and got the cell door open. Luckily, I came in *just* in the nick of time to stop an armed and dangerous fleeing fugitive."

Nate walked over and unlocked the cell door.

"Let's get it done, son," he said. "Sam Rafferty could be back as early as tomorrow."

"Get out here, Davis," Butch ordered.

Jimmy suddenly rallied. "Eat shit, you murdering bastard! I'm damned if I'll help you kill me."

"Just kill him where he sits," Nate snapped. "We'll drag the body out after and make the place look like there was a struggle."

Butch drew his big-bore Remington and thumb-cocked it.

"Here comes Jesus to cover you with a blanket," he said softly.

Butch was just taking up the trigger slack when the

street door banged open. A big, Irish-looking cavalry sergeant filled the doorway. A squad of armed troops stood behind him, rifles at port arms.

"Gentlemen," he announced in a booming voice of authority, "I'm Sergeant John Avery, Fourth Cavalry Regiment, Fort Union. Under the direct authority of the commanding officer at Fort Union, I now officially declare Springer to be under martial law. Stand down and surrender your weapons!"

It was early afternoon before Fargo got his first view of the ruined shell of Pecos.

It was a little cubbyhole of a village a few hours ride southeast of Santa Fe. Long before Fargo's day, the original Pecos Pueblo had been a place where Plains and Pueblo Indians met to swap goods. Then it was weakened by repeated Comanche and Apache raids.

Smallpox had been the final blow, and still plagued the few survivors of this virtual ghost town. By all accounts, that old prospector's included, the place was now an outlaw haven.

So Fargo rode among the cottonwoods framing the river, approaching slowly. Deerflies were pesky near the water and the annoyed Ovaro kept flipping his mane and tail to scatter them.

Fargo spotted the ruins of the adobe brick mission church, then a scattering of simple adobe dwellings. Some appeared abandoned, while others showed signs of tenants.

A huge, bleached jawbone protruded from a heap of ruins near the church—from what ancient creature, Fargo couldn't say. But it was one hell of a welcome to town.

"Let's go send in our card, boy," Fargo remarked to the Ovaro as they cleared the tree cover.

His brass-frame Henry was cocked and to hand, sixteen rounds in the tube magazine. Fargo figured he was flying the black flag now—this was not only a robber's roost, but Blaze Weston's trail led straight to it. The only "diplomacy" now would be backed by lead and gunsmoke.

Blaze's trail abruptly veered right, skirting the village.

Feeling vulnerable in the open, his eyes in constant scanning motion, Fargo followed the trail to an isolated adobe dwelling atop a low rise.

It was clear someone lived there—cooking odors lingered, and scrawny chickens picked for worms in the stony dirt of the front yard. Out back, laundry flapped eerily in the wind, strung from an old lariat tied between two paloverdes.

But what immediately caught and held Fargo's eye was the white towel hanging from the gate before the dwelling's mesquite-pole ramada—the warning sign that someone inside was afflicted with smallpox, stay away.

Or was that towel another one of Blaze Weston's creatively sick pranks? Because the signs were clear. Blaze had halted his horse, dismounted, and walked into the house. A second set of prints emerged. He'd mounted and ridden northwest, toward Santa Fe.

But what did he do inside that house?

Dread lay heavy in Fargo's belly as he swung down, landing light as a cat. He threw the reins, knowing the Ovaro would wait in place.

The wind whipped up to a howl, grit slapping at Fargo's face and in his eyes. The gate sprang free of its weak latch and began banging and flapping like loose roofing.

His finger curled around the trigger, Fargo slowly circled the place. Nothing out of the ordinary: Just a typical pueblo dwelling with a large brick *horno,* or oven, built behind the house for summer cooking. In the punishing Southwest heat, cooking had to be done outdoors.

Fargo bent low and rushed up to an unshuttered window opening, peeking inside.

At first, nothing unusual caught his notice. It was a simple, one-room dwelling with bare furnishings of rustic construction. There were wall pegs for a rifle rack on the opposite wall, but no weapons on it.

Then Fargo saw an old jackknife stuck into the middle of the wooden table—pinning down a note.

He vaulted through the window, took a deep breath, glanced down at the crude letters: "Look in the *horno,* Fargo."

Fargo's first response was fear, but a man couldn't

survive in its grip, and Fargo was a survivor. He reached down deep inside himself and got hold of the courage that was his by right of deed and honor. Skye Fargo held himself above no man, but neither had he ever met his better—and this sick spawn of everything evil was certainly no exception.

Even thus fortified, those few steps around to the back of the house made up the longest, bleakest walk of Fargo's life.

He paused before the *horno,* touched it, and realized it still felt warm.

His mind saw it all over: riding in, seeing the chickens, the laundry . . . and whiffing the lingering odor of cooking smells.

Reluctantly, he stood to one side and rolled away the round stone cover of the oven. The former tenant of the dwelling was now nothing but charred bones and still-smoldering ashes.

Fargo, seldom a weak-stomached man, was nonetheless forced to turn quickly away as he involuntarily retched. He was standing out in the open, sick and distracted, when a hammering racket of gunfire erupted.

Bullets chunked in all around him as Fargo realized his mistake. He was probably being fired at by the same rifle missing from the gun rack inside.

He knew he'd be sliced to wolf bait if he stayed on his feet and tried to make it back into the house. So Fargo tucked and rolled, desperately searching for muzzle flash or any sign of a target.

He lost a chunk of bootheel when a slug tagged it. But the direction in which the chunk flew off gave Fargo a general fix on Blaze's location: a sandy knoll about two hundred yards distant.

Fargo glimpsed a reflection and opened fire with a vengeance.

His mouth set hard, his lake blue eyes as determined as destiny, Fargo levered and fired as rapidly as he could while still holding a tight, effective pattern. Repeatedly the Henry's stock slapped his right cheek and bucked into his shoulder. When he emptied his magazine, the barrel was so hot Fargo could hear the gun oil sizzling.

In the ensuing silence, he could feel his ears ringing.

The acrid stench of gunpowder hovered in a blue, shifting mist over his position.

And then his ears picked up the sound—the rapid drumbeat of retreating hooves, from the far side of that knoll. Evidently, whatever repeating weapon Blaze stole from the house could not outlast the Henry's magazine capacity.

Weary, disgusted, yet glad to still be alive, Fargo returned to his stallion and somehow found the energy to, once again, swing up into leather.

"It ain't over till the hole card's played," Fargo reminded himself.

As Fargo pointed the Ovaro's bridle toward Santa Fe, one thought especially troubled him: Blaze Weston seemed more intent than before on killing him. Which naturally made Fargo wonder why Blaze needed him out of the way.

What big plan did Weston have in that putrid cesspool he called a brain?

12

The sun was westering, and Fargo's shadow growing long and thin as he followed the Old Pecos Trail north-west toward Santa Fe. The air was still and hot, the windmills he passed as motionless as paintings.

Many potential ambush points kept Fargo's tired, grit-irritated eyes in motion. He was especially careful when passing the huge chunks of sandstone that occasionally appeared along the trail.

And always, that nagging question: *What's his big plan?*

Fargo had to remain especially vigilant now, because Santa Fe drew a lot more traffic—and prying eyes—than did remote spots like Santa Cruz, Chimayo, or Pecos. Nor could he forget there was a U.S. marshal and dep-uty there.

About a mile south of Santa Fe, Fargo spotted a Pueblo Indian hoeing beans beside his adobe home.

"You look thirsty, *señor,*" the Pueblo called out to him.

Fargo reined in. "I'm spitting cotton," he admitted. He slapped his empty canteen. "Too much alkali in that Pecos water."

"Your fine horse needs water, also. We have cool well water here. *Mi casa es su casa.*"

" 'Preciate it," Fargo said, throwing off and leading his stallion off the trail.

"I call myself Cholla, *señor.* I am a Tewa from the Isleta Pueblo south of Albuquerque. My family and I were driven north by Apaches."

"Seen a few of them lately myself," Fargo said. "Dave is my name."

Fargo could hear an infant squalling from inside the house. Older children were also working in the fields.

"Thanks," he said when Cholla handed him a gourd filled with cool water.

Fargo drank deeply. The cool, sweet water landed in his belly like rain to dry earth.

"Strip your horse and water him from that stock trough," Cholla said, pointing to a crude stable and paddock out back. "Then bathe in the *acequia* and join us for our meal. You also need rest, *señor.*"

As much as Fargo hated to cut Weston any slack, the Tewa was right. Fargo had been nodding out in the saddle. And given the present danger he faced, that was a sure way to end up as carrion bait.

He stripped the Ovaro down to the neck leather, then spread the saturated saddle blanket out to dry in the last of the day's hot sun. Fargo walked to the nearby irrigation ditch and scrubbed and shaved, hating the feel of the razor scraping his cheeks.

During all this, he noticed something interesting. There was a fine-looking saddle horse in the stable—a chestnut stallion with a roached mane and two white socks. *Indios* were permitted to own dray animals, but this was clearly no plow nag.

While Cholla finished up in the fields, Fargo lay in the shade of a brush ramada before the house and got some badly needed sleep.

"That's some good horseflesh you got out back, Cholla," Fargo remarked later at supper.

The Tewa nodded proudly.

"At night sometimes I sneak him out for a ride, despite the laws. I break any law that is unjust. My family and I, we have bathed in *amole.*"

Fargo nodded, understanding. When a Christianized Indian scrubbed himself with *amole,* the root of the yucca plant, he was symbolically washing away his baptism and returning to his Indian beliefs.

"I could sure use a fine horse for a day or two," Fargo remarked casually, dipping the corner of a blue-corn tortilla into his wooden bowl of spiced beans.

Cholla's round face looked perplexed. "Señor Dave, you rode up today on the finest horse I have ever seen."

Yeah, thought Fargo, *which means he'll draw too much attention in Santa Fe.*

"I'd like to rest him up here," Fargo said. "Let him graze."

"You wish to borrow my chestnut?"

"Rent him," Fargo clarified. "If you'll take U.S. Script, that is."

Cholla thought about this. "How can it be a bad thing for me?" he reasoned. "You will leave a better horse than the one you take."

Fargo nodded.

"But I cannot lie," Cholla added. "This *is* a good horse. But the Mexican who begged me to take him off his hands called him only *hijo de puta,* son of a whore."

Cholla's wife cleared her throat to remind him that little pitchers have big ears—the six children seated at the long table were staring at this tall, blue-eyed Anglo as if he were a museum display.

"Bad temper?" Fargo asked.

"Not in the way you mean it, Dave. He is *ladino,* a sly one. Very cunning. He lulls the rider until the right moment, and then suddenly and viciously bucks him."

Cholla touched his left and right collar bones. "Each of these he has broken, as well as one of my ankles. Are you sure you might not prefer to ride your tired horse instead of a sly one?"

"I'll take my chances," Fargo said, the words meaning more than Cholla needed to know.

Blaze Weston.

The name hounded Fargo's thoughts as he made the final approach into Santa Fe just after sunset.

Given the clues, especially Rosalinda's description of her encounter with Weston, Fargo had a gut fear he couldn't ignore.

It struck the Trailsman as no great mystery why a sick fanatic like Weston might take his "purification by fire" to Santa Fe. Its name might mean "city of the holy faith." But there was also plenty that was unholy, to some, about this ancient place where tolerance and recreation went hand in hand.

To Fargo, Santa Fe was a place to have some harmless fun after a long, hard journey to get there. But what did it seem like filtered through the lens of a mind like Weston's?

Rules of propriety were much more relaxed in wide-open Santa Fe. Even proper young ladies from the "best" families were seen smoking tobacco and drinking liquor in public. And local fashion currently bared so much breast that some new female arrivals fainted at the first shocking sight. Their husbands, however, seemed to withstand the shock with no great effort, Fargo had noticed.

But how, Fargo wondered again, was all this playing in Weston's mind? Then again, Weston was not always predictable.

The chestnut was behaving fine so far, and Fargo drew little notice in the darkness as he entered the lively town. He trotted past El Palacio, better known as the Mud Palace. Unimpressive, overall, but the oldest public building in the United States.

Fargo watched doorways, alleys. Lights blazed everywhere, revealing how most of the adobe buildings were plastered white and topped by red tile roofs. Fargo had watched Indian women make such tiles by shaping them on their thighs.

"Psst! Hey, handsome!"

Fargo glanced into the liquid yellow light pouring from a saloon. A sporting gal watched him from painted eyes.

"How 'bout I lick some sugar from your tummy—for starters?" she invited.

Fargo reined in and touched his hat. "Married man," he lied.

She laughed, shooting twin streams of smoke through her nostrils. She was smoking a dark little cigar.

"So what? Honey, my *husband* changes the sheets after."

Fargo searched out the name of the place, for they all blended together in his mind. He found the name emblazoned in gilt letters under a lantern: THE THREE SISTERS. He recalled it as one of the wilder spots in Santa

Fe. Just the kind of place that might interest a "purifier" like Blaze Weston—especially since it was one of the few wooden structures in town.

Fargo rode past, tied off the chestnut, and followed the boardwalk back to the Three Sisters. The street out front would be too hoof-packed to find sign, so he slipped between buildings and went around back of the saloon.

It took only a few minutes searching to find the hob-nailed boot prints.

Just seeing them made it feel like lice were crawling all over Fargo's scalp.

He went back out to the street and searched out the broadsides.

MANHUNT WIDENS EVEN AS FARGO'S ACCUSED
ACCOMPLICE RELEASED!!!

A little grin spread Fargo's lips. At least Major Carlson had come through in time.

He slowly strolled the boardwalks on both sides, sticking to the shadows and watching everyone from wary eyes. That's how he spotted a familiar figure emerging from the La Paloma cafe.

The man was silver-haired and heavyset, a strong man growing soft as age claimed him. He wore a rawhide vest with a star pinned to it. He walked with the clumsy gait of men who've spent much of their youth sleeping on hard, cold ground and now have some rust in their hinges.

Fargo followed him to a boardinghouse on Commerce Street. The man went round to a rear door. He was just keying the lock when Fargo poked the Colt's muzzle into his ribs.

"Jesus Christ, I'm getting old," the man muttered in a voice rough as eighty-grit sandpaper. "Wallet's tucked into my boot."

"No, it ain't, Sam Rafferty, you silver fox. You'll carry a wallet when I become a barber's clerk. You just mean to mule-kick me when I bend down for it."

The sheriff of Springer still hadn't turned around.

"Hmm . . . you know my name, and I know that

voice," he said. "Since you ain't shot me by now, you can't be some skunk I sent to prison."

"Go on inside. I'm a little nervous, right now, standing in one spot too long. There's a jasper been notching sights on me lately."

"If this is how you conduct your affairs," Sam groused as he opened the door to his room, "I can see how you'd be nervous."

Sam fired up a lantern, turned the wick way up, then turned to confront his captor.

He had to stare for several seconds before recognition gleamed in his eyes.

"Bleedin' Holy Ghost! Fargo, are you a damn fool?"

Fargo debated whether or not to leather his Colt. He and Rafferty were not exactly friends, though their paths had crossed several times over the years.

He took a chance and dropped his Colt into the holster. "Sam, you don't for one minute believe what you've been reading and hearing about me, do you?"

The grizzled old marshal snorted.

" 'Course not—it's hogwash. I've known you to brawl, and you chase more tail than ten men. You'll end up butt-shot while diving out a bedroom window someday, and serve you right. But you ain't got a criminal bone in you."

"Thanks."

"Thank a cat's tail! Goddammit, Fargo, I don't like it when a man draws down on me."

Fargo's head suddenly rocked back when the old lawman hit him. It wasn't a punch with much behind it—just enough to even the score.

"Square deal?" Sam demanded.

Fargo rubbed his jaw and nodded. "Square deal."

"All right, what the hell's going on in Springer? Today I hear soldiers took the damn town over."

"Damn right, and at my request."

"At *your* re—" Sam went red in the face. He unpinned his badge. "Hell, take it, Fargo. Might as well, if you're gonna ramrod the place."

"Simmer down, Sam. Hell, it saved a man's life."

Rafferty's anger turned to astonishment as Fargo quickly filled him in on the details. The arrival of Blaze Weston, the secret meeting between Nate Robinson and

Blaze. The frame-up of Jimmy Davis in an effort to destroy competition for Nate's brick business.

"The thing is," Fargo concluded, "you still have to get back there quick even with the arrival of the soldiers. The Army doesn't know any of this about Nate and Butch. They could rabbit at any time."

"I was heading back tomorrow anyhow," Rafferty assured him. "The trial here is wrapped up."

Fargo cleared his throat. "Before you go, any chance I might put the touch on you? I'm mighty light in the pockets."

"What, to keep you in whores and whiskey? Any money I part with better be for official business. It gets billed to the town."

"It's so I can hang on long enough to stop Blaze Weston from burning down half the territory. You think I got time right now to set rabbit snares so I can eat? Is killing Weston official enough for you?"

Rafferty grunted in the affirmative and flipped him a single eagle gold piece.

He paused, again mulling all Fargo had told him.

"Blaze Weston," he repeated. "And Nate Robinson behind it—*hell* yes! I always did believe the stories about how that son of a bitch led a scalper army down south back in the Forties. But that was out of my jurisdiction."

Sam unbuckled his gun belt and hung it on one of the bedposts.

"I always suspected, too, that he was using that blood money to set himself up as a big nabob in the territory. But I never *had* anything on him."

"Well, Nate and Butch have both fouled their nest this time," Fargo said. "Just put some pressure on a fellow named Josh and a few others on the Vigilance Committee—they'll give you plenty if it's them or the Robinsons. No loyalty in that bunch."

"Brother, I intend to. They'll swing, Nate and Butch both. For a fact they will."

Fargo reached for the doorknob. "Nate, maybe. In Butch's case, I may be saving the good citizens of Springer the cost of a rope."

"Personal, huh?"

Fargo nodded.

Rafferty grunted. "You know the rule in the Territories, Fargo. You'll be in no trouble so long as the bullet hole's in the front."

"They always are," Fargo assured him before closing the door behind himself.

Santa Fe was known for staying lively well into the night. Fargo knew Weston well enough by now not to make any assumptions. Those prints, behind the Three Sisters saloon and whorehouse, could have been deliberately planted to keep Fargo stationed there.

So, instead, he stayed on the move. Fargo nursed a whiskey here, a coffee there, patrolled the streets and alleys on foot.

As much as possible he stuck to the shadows. It was around eleven P.M. and he was just emerging from his latest check of the alley beside the Three Sisters. Fargo literally collided with a young U.S. deputy marshal.

"Hell," Fargo muttered, acting a little drunk, "my fault. Beg pardon, deputy."

The deputy surveyed him from suspicious eyes.

"You new to town, fella?"

Fargo laughed. He hooked a thumb toward the top floor of the saloon.

"Go ask Rosie if I'm new. That greedy cashbox has been taking my savings for too damn long now."

It had never failed Fargo yet—as sure as sunset, there was always a "Rosie" in any whorehouse in the West.

The deputy's face slacked into a grin. "Serves you right. Now Annie's the one gets my money. *That* filly can buck. No offense, friend, but Rosie looks like she's been rode hard and put away wet once too often."

The deputy laughed and then drifted on, and Fargo expelled a long sigh.

By midnight, most establishments were closed or clearing out, and the streets virtually deserted. Fargo figured the law wouldn't likely be patrolling now—with only two men, they had to sleep sometime.

Periodically, Fargo had been returning to keep an eye on the Three Sisters—that's how he detected new prints made by Blaze Weston.

Fresh prints . . . made during Fargo's last check around the rest of the town.

He shucked out his Colt, thumb-cocked it, and slipped around to the empty weed lot behind the building.

Nothing. Just the hum of insects and the mourning of the wind. Fargo sniffed, detecting no coal-oil smell. It had made the air reek inside the chapel in Santa Cruz. That was some reassurance.

Still . . . Fargo recalled how those Pueblos had responded to his questions about Weston, fear of hell itself in their eyes. How the man seemed to leave a lingering trace of evil in the very air—a cold, tickling presence that tightened the scalp and stiffened the hairs on Fargo's arms.

Just like right now.

"Up and on the line, Fargo," he rallied himself. "He'll bleed red like all the rest."

Carefully, he worked his way around the entire building, searching for signs that it had been rigged for incineration. He found nothing, and lost Blaze's latest prints on the boardwalk.

Fargo gazed out at the suddenly lonely night, frustrated anew. He could only be in one place at a time, so *which* place was most important?

This could just be a diversion. Get Fargo locked onto one building, then fire up another. But he couldn't risk ignoring the clues. After all, Weston obviously had a vendetta against women in particular—and here was a building full of them.

So finally Fargo picked a dark corner out back and settled in for a long stint of guard duty.

When the sun finally broke over the nearby mountains, with no signs of any fire during the night, relief washed over a hungry and tired Skye Fargo.

He was the day's first patron at the La Paloma cafe. Fargo tied into a hearty breakfast of eggs *relleno* and spicy *chorizo* sausage, washed down with black coffee.

He was holding his cup out for a refill when a tongue of black smoke licked past the open front doors— carrying the scent of scorched wood with it.

"That *bastard*!"

Fargo's cup shattered when he dropped it, his chair flew, toppling over as he raced out into the street.

There! From the far edge of town, billows of black smoke filled the air, accompanied by crackling flames.

The chestnut was still tied off in front of the saloon. Fargo hit leather, tugged rein, and went galloping at breakneck speed toward the fire. He couldn't understand all that smoke until he identified the smell of creosote—wood oiled with creosote gave off thick smoke when burned. Only now were the first shouts of alarm going up throughout the newly risen town.

The smoke kept Fargo from seeing, at first, what was actually on fire. There were several private dwellings clustered there, and he assumed it must be one of the houses.

But as he drew abreast of the conflagration, confusion set in.

The wind had shifted the smoke, and he could see that no structure was burning nor even in danger. Only an old stack of railroad ties stored well behind the cluster of houses. That explained the creosote smell, all the smoke.

But why would Weston bother—

Fargo caught sudden motion from the corner of his left eye. He slewed in the saddle just enough to bring himself face-to-face with Blaze Weston, astride a big sorrel. They had just debouched from a side alley, and Blaze Weston had his stolen repeating rifle already locked into his shoulder.

In a heartbeat Fargo realized: This entire night, those decoy boot prints, the harmless fire set as a feint—all designed for this moment, and the demise of Skye Fargo.

Even as Blaze opened up with an unholy vengeance, Fargo kicked his feet out of the stirrups, pitched himself backward, and literally did a backflip over the rump of the chestnut.

He landed in the dirt, came up on his heels as his Colt cleared leather, and started fanning the hammer.

Hot lead crossed the wide dirt street from both directions, a furious fusillade that shattered the peace of the morning. The panicked chestnut kept tossing sand in

Fargo's face as it kicked and reared, so all he could do was spray his shots while also avoiding the horse's hooves.

Fargo expected to meet his maker with every detonation of Weston's rifle. But all that dust, and Blaze's own nervously jumping horse, must have saved him. Because, finally, Fargo heard Blaze's hammer fall on an empty chamber.

Blaze slapped the sorrel's rump, and they galloped out of town, headed north.

Now it's over, Fargo vowed to himself, grabbing the chestnut's reins to get him under control.

That road north was nearly straight for at least four miles, with steep rock walls and plenty of rock tumbles to prevent any sneak turnoffs. Weston had only one way to go. True, Fargo sorely missed his dependable Ovaro. But the chestnut was well rested and Fargo's Henry had plenty of effective range and plenty of rounds.

This was definitely a justified case of *ley fuga,* and Fargo would gladly shoot this monster in the back. One thing for sure, there was no heart to aim for.

He hit a stirrup, vaulted into leather, then thumped the chestnut soundly with his heels. Only then, when it was too damn late to matter, did Fargo recall Cholla's warning about the chestnut:

The Mexican who begged me to take him called him only hijo de puta, *son of a whore. He is* ladino, *sly and cunning.*

The moment Fargo thumped the chestnut's ribs, it nickered in triumphant rebellion. Quick as a finger snap, the horse hunkered on its hocks, then leaped almost vertically into the air, coming down on its back to crush the rider.

Only by a deft, last-second twist did Fargo avoid a broken back. He crashed hard into the dirt street, dazed, the wind knocked out of him.

As he lay there, cursing and sucking wind, he watched the chestnut bolt away on its own, taking Fargo's tack and Henry with him.

And far worse, making sure Blaze Weston would escape to kill again.

13

By the time Fargo made it to his feet, rattled but not seriously hurt, Santa Fe was no longer a slumbering city.

The fierce gun battle, the cries of fire, the still billowing clouds of smoke—suddenly the street was boiling with activity, all of it pouring in his direction.

And there'll be at least two badges in that crowd, Fargo reminded himself.

He wasn't stupid enough to add horse-stealing to his long list of troubles, so Fargo slipped behind the houses, then headed out of town at a dead run to see if he could wrangle that damned rented horse from hell.

Fortunately, the chestnut was hungry, and smart enough to know it was his rider who fed him. Fargo found him standing in the road about a mile out of town, nibbling some pine needles.

Fargo kept his tone gentle and persuasive, softly coaxing, as he slowly approached the double-poxed *ladino* chestnut. Anyone overhearing Fargo, however, would have been shocked by the difference between tone and words.

"You goddamned worthless tub of guts and glue," he said sweetly, tempted to shoot the four-legged son of a bitch on the spot. "That's a good bastard, easy now, you equestrian whore."

The chestnut flipped its mane, eyeing Fargo warily.

"Hell yes, I'd shoot you," Fargo cooed in a lover's tone. "Shoot you, cook you, and spoon-feed you to those Apaches watching us. You spavined nag, if you ever want to wear an oat bag again, hold still."

The chestnut's vocabulary must have been limited, for

only seconds later, he let Fargo mount. The stallion doc-
ilely responded when Fargo tugged rein and headed
north.

He cursed at his luck, for he couldn't begin pursuing
Weston again until he retrieved his Ovaro. And, since
Cholla lived south of Santa Fe, Fargo had to waste valu-
able time doubling back and circling wide of town. He
could hardly go trotting boldly through Santa Fe now,
after scores of witnesses saw him flee from the fire.

On top of all that, he had no idea when this crazy
damned man-killer would try to crush him again.

"Pile on the agony," Fargo muttered.

Gently, he patted the chestnut's neck to assure him
they were pals, secretly fantasizing about riding it
straight to a rendering plant.

"How was my horse?" Cholla greeted Fargo as he
rode into the Tewa's yard late in the morning.

"Hell on four sticks," Fargo shot back. "That ain't no
stallion—it's a mare. A goddamn *nightmare.*"

He swung down, still scowling, and rapidly began
stripping off his tack.

Cholla set aside his hoe, looking surprised.

"You would like your money back, Dave?"

"Nah," Fargo said. "It ain't that. But, hell, Cholla,
you only said that critter is a bucker. Christ, it tried to
kill me. Chinned the moon and tried to break my back."

"Dave, that cannot be, this—"

Cholla paused and suddenly looked guilty. "Señor
Dave, you did not leave him saddled all night, did you?"

Fargo, finished stripping the tack, stared at the Tewa.
"Matter fact, I did. Why?"

"*Soy un necio!* I am a fool! I forgot to tell you—he
turns especially vicious if he has been left saddled and
unridden. Apparently, he resents this."

"*Resents* it?" Fargo shook his head in disgust. "Oh,
so he's *temperamental*? Well, pardon me all to hell for
mistaking the princess for a damned horse. That
bastard."

"Actually," Cholla corrected him, "his name is Son of
a Whore."

"It's usually all one."

Fargo was never so glad in his life to see the Ovaro again. At least the stallion was well fed and rested.

Fargo headed north again, skirting Santa Fe along the Madrid Trail. It was easy to pick up Blaze's path again, although by now he was many hours ahead of Fargo.

Weston was presently headed north—that's all Fargo could tell for now. If his course remained more or less due north, one likely destination was that sawmill in the sacred valley. If his course shifted northeast, he might be returning to Springer. Maybe to check in with Nate Robinson for further orders.

Hell, who knows, with him? Fargo thought. One thing was damn sure in the Trailsman's mind: Blaze Weston had a master plan of his own. And if somebody didn't stop him, despite all this murder and mayhem so far, the worst was yet to come.

Thanks to a new railroad spur between Santa Fe and Springer, Sheriff Sam Rafferty was not forced to take the Bone Crusher Express—an open-sided wagon that made the trip in two teeth-rattling days.

Instead, late in the afternoon of the same day he left, he detrained at Springer.

With his arrival, the state of martial law was lifted and the soldiers dismissed. When Sam got one look at the bruised and banged-up Jimmy Davis, his blood boiled.

It was Esteban Robles who answered his angry knock on the Robinsons' front door.

"Nate to home?" the lawman demanded. "And that worthless punk kid of his?"

"Sam!" Nate Robinson called out in his booming, hail-fellow-well-met voice. He stood in the hallway behind Esteban. "Welcome back!"

Rafferty pushed his solid bulk past Esteban.

"T'hell with the welcomes, Nate. I want to know what in Sam Hill you and your boy think you're doing? I just took Jimmy Davis over to Doc Crowley's."

"Oh? Jimmy's not feeling well?"

"Don't try to hornswoggle me, Nate. He's got broken teeth, cracked ribs, and bruises over most of his body. And he says your boy put most of them there while others held him down."

Nate made a gesture of dismissal. "Of course he'll say anything to minimize his guilt. Butch tells me he resisted arrest."

"*Arrest?* On what evidence or authority?"

"A citizen's arrest, that's the authority. Perfectly legal in the absence of any law. And the evidence was found in his hotel room."

"That shit the maid claims to have found was planted—that's obvious as clown makeup."

"Oh?" Nate raised his eyebrows. "Planted by whom, Sam?"

Rafferty could see the flap holster under Robinson's frock coat. The lawman rested the heel of his right palm on the butt of his Paterson Colt.

"Tell you what. Let's let *me* be the sheriff," he suggested in a tone that made it clear he was taking over. "And *you* answer some questions."

Nate gave one of his trademark toothy smiles, all affability. "Of course, Sam, by all means. I'm a law-abiding citizen."

"Uh-huh. So tell me, Mr. Law-abiding Citizen, why would you be having a secret meeting with the likes of Blaze Weston?"

Nate had been an accomplished liar all of his life. But this question caught him broadside. For the space of a few heartbeats, his face paled.

"Who?" he finally repeated. "Can't say I know that name."

Rafferty grunted. "If you don't know it, you must live with your head up your ass, Nate. Blaze Weston is an arsonist. The motherless scut has killed scores of people, including a bunch of orphans."

"Sounds like a terrible man," Nate remarked, his obsidian eyes growing cold and hard.

"So low he could walk under a snake's belly on stilts," Rafferty agreed. "Now you tell me—what would that make any man who hired him for his services?"

"Why, a dastardly criminal, of course. That's why we arrested Jimmy Davis—on evidence that he either hired Skye Fargo or is working in league with him."

"Jesus, you make me puke, Robinson, you know that?

Just looking at a filthy maggot like you sours my stomach. You've bluffed everybody for years with your book talk and fancy feathers. But you went too far this time. I ain't got the evidence yet to cuff you. But, mister, it's coming like a cannonball."

"Use a pillow," Nate said.

Rafferty, about to turn around and stomp out of the house, looked perplexed.

"A pillow?" he repeated. "The hell you—?"

Nate stepped quickly to one side.

"Señor Rafferty!" Esteban's voice shouted. "Behind you!"

But his warning came too late. Butch Robinson, a satin sofa pillow wrapped around his Remington, shot the sheriff in the back of the head at almost point-blank range. Rafferty's body thumped lifeless to the floor, his toes scratching the carpet a few times as his nervous system tried to deny the cold, hard, sudden fact of death.

The pillow had muffled the shot from any passersby out on Copper Street. But Bobbie Jean, busy cleaning Cynthia's upstairs wing of the house, heard it and came running to the balustrade on the landing. When she saw Rafferty dead on the floor, blood still pluming from the back of his head, she screamed.

Butch swung the still-smoking muzzle of his Remington toward her. "Down here *now,* bitch! And none of your usual goddamn lip, or you'll get what Rafferty just got."

Next he swung the gun toward Esteban.

"And you, Sancho—go sit over on the sofa with Bobbie Jean. Either of you two get cute, I'll blow you to perdition."

When their servants were safely out of earshot, Butch said urgently, "Christ! The son of a bitch knew everything, Pa. How'd he piece all that together down in Santa Fe?"

"How do you think, you bonehead?" Nate snapped. "Skye Fargo. He's the only one could have known."

Nate stepped aside to avoid getting blood on his new calfskin boots. They cost twenty dollars and came all the way from St. Louis.

For Butch, it was just settling in to his mind that he had killed the popular sheriff of Springer. Panic took over his surly features.

"God *damn* you, old man!" he exploded. "Why in hell did you hafta drag Blaze Weston into it? Christ, we're up Salt River now."

"This is no time to go puny," Nate berated him. "Rafferty is dead, right? The only other person who's put it together is Skye Fargo. And we know, from the latest report by Steve Kitchens, that Fargo is now trailing Blaze in this direction."

"Yeah, so what?"

Nate nodded toward the supine body.

"After dark, we haul that carcass out of here. We can use one of our freight wagons, make it look like a delivery run. We get a bunch of boys from the Vigilance Committee to swear along with us that we all saw *Fargo* kill Rafferty."

Butch's worried frown was replaced by a nervy little grin. "That's the gait! And then me and some a the boys ride out to intercept Fargo. I fill him with lead, and we're in a bonanza."

Nate smiled. "Now *that's* my lad! *Pecca fortiter,* Butchie boy. It's Latin for 'sin bravely.'"

Esteban coughed, from the parlor, and Butch looked worried again.

"Shit," he said. "Cynthia's at the emporium, so she's no witness to anything that happened here. But we still got two witnesses who know I killed Rafferty."

Nate nodded. "They're a low priority right now. We'll take them into the cellar and truss and gag 'em good. Right now, though, it's Fargo we need to concentrate on. Then we'll haul those other two off and kill them, dispose of the bodies. Indentured servants run away all the time."

"Bobbie Jean ain't going to waste before I kill her," Butch vowed.

"Never suggested she should, did I? I'll taste that stuff myself," Nate agreed. "Hell, all the boys can take a whack at her as an extra reward for their good work."

Butch grinned. "Hell, yeah. Ain't no stud in town don't want to top that filly."

"But first things first," Nate reminded him. "Get the boys together and ready to ride. I'll have Esteban clean up this mess and help me hide Rafferty's body for now. Then I'll tie up those two downstairs."

Butch started to turn away, then paused.

"What about Blaze Weston?" he asked.

"What do you mean?"

"The crazy bastard is still out there stoking fires, that's what I mean."

Nate shrugged an indifferent shoulder. "None of our picnic, is it? With all the witnesses dead, who can link us to him? Hell, *let* him rip. It's more business for us."

By an hour before sunset, Fargo was sure Weston was headed back to Springer.

Blaze had veered northeast while still well south of Taos and the sacred valley. He was moving fast, stopping seldom. The actions of a man with a purpose. And the ultimate nature of that purpose scared the snot out of Fargo even without his knowing exactly what it was.

The pointed brim of his hat cast his face in shadow as he cleared the Sangre de Cristo range and rode into the rolling foothill country of northeastern New Mexico. Fargo glanced around at the terrain, not liking it. If Weston had decided to hole up, lay in wait, and make another ambush attempt, this was ideal country for it.

Fargo would far prefer the open country—the redrock expanse of the Navajo homeland, even the bleached alkali wasteland of the Jornada del Muerto. Saltbrush, yucca, and cactus provided far less cover than cottonwoods, rock spines, and rimrock.

Nor could Fargo forget that Blaze Weston wasn't his only problem. Right now Skye Fargo was fugitive number one in the territory, and every nickel-novel "hero" within miles was hoping to become legend by sending him under.

And then there was also Fargo's now-constant shadow, that Apache outlaw band.

They were watching him even now, and they'd been watching him all day. Fargo wasn't sure why, and with Apaches he wouldn't even waste time guessing motives. Since Fargo had shot that brave's fingertip off, they had showed him the respect of not crowding him again. But they were always there in the distance, sticking to the high ground. Now and then, when the wind was just right, Fargo could even hear them singing the ancient songs. No words, just tones, for to Indians the voice was a musical instrument that expressed feelings far beyond the power of mere words.

"They definitely got their eyes in this direction, old campaigner," Fargo told the Ovaro, who pricked up his ears. "And chances are good it's you they're most interested in."

Most Apaches wouldn't even waste a bullet on a white man—they killed them with rocks as they might a snake. Despite the real danger they represented, Fargo couldn't help admiring much about them. Their lives were harsh, but Apaches kept their word and disdained fear. They had always rejected "organizing" as a people, each group independent and settling its own disputes without appeal to "higher authority."

Exactly the way Fargo liked to live.

The sun was half sunk behind the mountains when Fargo topped a low rise and spotted an old shack, its walls patched with flattened tin cans.

"Hallo, the shack!" he called out before riding closer.

"Hallo back atcha, stranger!"

The voice was old, pleghmy, tobacco-roughened. Fargo watched the double barrels of a twelve-gauge shotgun come easing out the front door.

"You here to rob me, too, mister?" the voice demanded.

Fargo nodded toward a big wooden rainwater casket at one corner of the shack. The lid dangled from its rope tether.

"All I care to rob you for is enough water to stay my horse's belly, that's all."

The owner of the gun stepped out behind it, eyeing him cautiously. He had at least twenty-five years on Fargo, and had to squint to make him out.

"Ain't never turned a man down yet," he replied. "Nor sent one away hungry, neither. Throw the bridle, son, and let that pinto drink his fill."

" 'Preciate it."

As he swung down, Fargo said, "What's this about being robbed?"

"Goddamnedest thing," the old salt told him, lowering his weapon. "I's out checking my traps just a little bit ago. Somebody went inside my shack, all right, on account it was all tossed up to shit, like a twister come through. But he only took two things: a can of kerosene and an old throwing knife."

"Kerosene," Fargo repeated, his face going cold.

"Yup, ain't that the shits? Hell, he ignored this scattergun and some damn good furs I mean to sell in Santa Fe. Stupid bastard."

Not stupid, thought Fargo. *Just crazy. And a killer.*

"And a throwing knife, huh?" he asked. Fargo recalled how accurately Blaze had thrown that infected knife at him. Of course—a bullet was too boring a way for Weston to dispatch a man.

The old coot nodded. "Nothing fancy. It's got a long, skinny blade with a sharp point. Meant for sinking in deep at close tossin' range. I won it off a Mexer down in El Paso in a game of stud. Mostly I just toss it at the door when it gets boresome."

The Ovaro finished drinking, and Fargo started to snug his bridle again.

"Dark's comin' on," the old man observed. "And these hills ain't no place to wander after sunset. You're welcome to pass the night here. Got a pot of stew simmering and a jug of Taos Lightning that'll put your dick in the dirt."

Fargo had smelled the stew when he rode up, and his mouth watered for some. All day long he'd been thinking about the cook in that cafe in Santa Fe, cutting biscuit rounds with a tin cup. Fargo hadn't properly finished that meal before the fire broke out, nor had he taken food since.

"I'd love to take you up on that, old-timer," Fargo said, swinging up into leather. "And I could use a good drunk right about now. But I've got to git."

"Suit yourself—it's a young man's world. But was I you? I wouldn't spread my blankets anywheres near here. There's Apaches prowling the area. Pure quill Apaches, the rough ones."

Fargo nodded. "I know. But believe me, there's far worse on the loose than rough Apaches."

A rising moon lighted the very tips of the mountains behind Fargo like silver patina. That generous moon-wash made riding easier, but also made him an easier target.

He was still only a little more than halfway to Springer, and even riding all night he wouldn't arrive until well into the day tomorrow.

Ever since talking to the old man, Fargo suspected Blaze had made a stop somewhere along the trail. Some ideal location perfect for an ambush.

Blaze *had* to stop Fargo so he would have a free hand for his master plan. Fargo couldn't prove there *was* such a plan, but he knew it the way animals sensed bad weather coming.

He entered a particularly risky stretch of trail. It was sheltered on both sides by frequent *bosquecillos,* small clumps of trees common to this region. His Henry was already to hand.

The wind shrieked, the Ovaro pricked up his ears, and Fargo thumbed his hammer from half to full cock.

"You out there, you sick son of a bitch?" Fargo challenged out loud.

He hadn't expected an answer. But the harsh, airy, grating voice that responded from the darkness turned his blood backwards in his veins.

"I'm *always* out here, Fargo! You're already dead! See you in hell!"

Thuck!

White-hot pain razor-traced a line across the back of Fargo's neck as the knife nicked him in passing, then embedded itself several inches deep into the bole of a tree beside him. So powerfully was it thrown, the haft still vibrated.

Bushes rustled on the opposite side of the trail—Weston escaping. Fargo saw moving branches, threw his Henry into his shoulder, and opened fire, peppering the position with lead.

He emptied half the magazine, the Henry's ejector clicking as hot brass shell casings rained down around him. But if he'd hit his mark, he hadn't dropped him. Fargo could still hear the sounds of escape, including fading, mocking laughter.

Fargo let the hammer down to half-cock and spoke to the Ovaro, calming him. Then he ripped some moss from a tree, packed it onto his burning neck, and tied it off with his bandanna.

"Sick or not," he said softly to himself, "that bastard is rawhide tough."

Fargo refilled the Henry's tube magazine, quickly ran a wiping patch through the bore, and then man and beast slogged on.

But it had been a long, hard day for Fargo, following an entire night of wakeful vigilance patrolling Santa Fe. And the last sleep he'd enjoyed had been a catnap under the ramada at Cholla's house.

Realizing he was too exhausted for constant vigilance, Fargo decided to make a cold camp and sleep a few hours. He selected a little clearing, well off the trail, surrounded by a protective deadfall of old, tangled brush and trees.

The deadfall was so thick that he had to throw off and lead his stallion in by the bridle reins. But that very fact was Fargo's natural sentry. No one, not even night shadow Blaze Weston, could penetrate this position without alerting him and the Ovaro.

Fargo stripped the pinto to the neck leather, rubbed him down, and watered him from his hat. Then, as an added precaution, he not only put the Ovaro on a short ground tether, he tied the reins around his wrist before crawling into his blankets. His weapons were both cocked and ready to hand.

Fargo didn't just fall asleep—he passed out quicker than a miner after a Saturday-night drunk. His dreams were a disturbed confusion of sounds and images. One moment La Llorona, the Weeping Woman, was only New Mexico's famous and ghostly wind; the next, La Llorona was a real woman named Elena Vargas, her weeping turning into screams of indescribable agony.

On your watch, Fargo. On your watch.

Fargo's dreamscape included the town of Springer, lit by a lurid orange glow. And the livery barn in Chico

137

Springs, flames licking high into the sky, popping, crackling, filling the air with an acrid stench . . .

A sharp tug at his wrist, the nervous Ovaro waking him, took Fargo from disturbing dreams to a waking nightmare.

Intense flames completely encircled him and the Ovaro! That "protective" deadfall had also provided deadly tinder for Blaze Weston's latest fire.

The flames were closing in like rapidly rising flood water, and Fargo could literally feel the heat.

Willing himself calm, he grabbed the wide-eyed Ovaro around the neck and spoke low in his ear, gentling the horse. Moving with machine precision, Fargo tossed on the saddle, cinched it quick, booted his Henry and holstered his Colt. Then he kicked out the picket pin and searched desperately for the safest way out of this fiery deathtrap.

But once again Blaze had done his work with deadly precision. There was an unbroken ring of fire all around them, and deadly, choking smoke closing in to suffocate them.

Which left only one decision: Fargo picked what appeared to be the narrowest point of the fire. Then he launched himself into the saddle, lowered his profile and center of balance, and raked his heels over the stallion's ribs.

The Ovaro knew, by the way his master loosened the reins to give him his head, that they were going to have to try to leap their way out of this one. As they raced toward their flaming escape point, Fargo felt the stallion lowering his hind quarters, gathering muscle for the jump.

We won't clear it, Fargo realized only seconds before they went airborne. The Ovaro was an excellent jumper and could clear the top rail of any fence Fargo had encountered. But this burning debris was higher—and much wider—than a fence.

"Hi-ya!" Fargo shouted, imitating the yipping war cry of the Northern Cheyennes. "Hiii-*ya*!"

He had put his mouth right next to the Ovaro's ear for this rallying cry. Now Fargo added what he hoped would be the saving touch: He gave the Ovaro a short, but sharp, bite to the most tender part of his ear.

Nothing enraged a horse more than a cold bit unless it was a bite to the ear. Nickering in fury, the magnificent stallion leaped with the launch power of a catapult.

For a few moments, Fargo felt like he was raw meat on a hot spit. Choking smoke clogged his eyes, nose, throat, and he was convinced they were going to plummet smack into inescapable hellfire.

The next moment, they cleared the burning deadfall, and landed on safe ground. The Ovaro, still miffed at Fargo for that bite, promptly bucked him off to teach him a lesson.

Fargo landed on his ass, the second time in one day he'd been tossed. But it never felt so good to be bucked.

"Sorry about the bite, old warhorse," Fargo said as he picked himself up and brushed off his hated dungarees. "But it was either that or be roasted alive."

Not a horse to harbor a grudge, the Ovaro nuzzled Fargo's shoulder to tell him all was forgiven.

Fargo was still thanking his lucky stars when the low, harsh, guttural voice shouted from the nearby darkness: "Like I said . . . I'm *always* out here, Fargo!"

14

Nate Robinson knew his wife was a creature of habit. Every night she drank herself into a stupor by ten P.M. No way on God's earth would she be aware of any noises coming from the cellar.

Especially not tonight, for he had slipped a healthy dose of laudanum into her flask.

Nate waited until Butch, following their earlier plan, had gathered up some of his fellow vigilantes and left to intercept Skye Fargo, hauling Sheriff Rafferty's body with them. Then Nate grabbed a lantern and headed down into the cellar.

Bobbie Jean Davis had been very much on his mind for a long time. And he'd never have a better opportunity than right now.

She and Esteban had been bound and gagged, then dragged into the separate little room used as a wine cellar.

"There's my happy domestic servants," he greeted them, his Colt Navy in hand.

He set the lantern down. Bobbie Jean didn't like the sheen in his eyes as his gaze devoured her like a flesh banquet.

"I'm going to remove your gags," he told them in his falsely affable tone. "But here's how it works: Whichever one of you is foolish enough to shout or scream, I'll kill the *other* one."

"What are you going to do with us?" Bobbie Jean demanded the moment her gag was removed.

Nate laughed. "Believe me, dear, there's definitely *one*

thing I'll be doing with you that I won't be doing with Esteban."

"Filthy swine," Esteban said behind him.

"You'll regret that insult, old man," Nate assured him without even turning around. He was too fascinated by the sight of Bobbie Jean, all delicious and helpless before him. And Butch thought he was going to get to it first!

He dropped to his knees and lowered his face close to hers. Bobbie Jean tried to turn her head away in disgust, but Nate cupped her chin in a hand like a steel trap and stopped her. He was surprisingly strong for a man well into his forties.

"That sweet, sweet mouth of yours," he told her, his voice going husky with lust. "Lips like two luscious little berries. Juicy berries. Always wanted to kiss that mouth."

"You do," she warned him, "and I'll bite your damn tongue off!"

"Oh, will you, Roberta?"

Bobbie Jean had never heard such an awful sound in her life as the metallic *snick* when he cocked the handgun. He poked the muzzle into her abdomen.

"You hurt me," he said, "I hurt you. See how simple that works? And *my* hurt hurts more."

The cold steel probing into her had transformed Bobbie Jean's anger to a bone-numbing fear. Repulsed, yet deathly afraid, she let him take full possession of her mouth. She felt like vomiting.

"*Now* you've got me nicely warmed up," he told her, starting to untie her ropes. "No sense in my putting it away angry, is there?"

"Leave her alone, you filthy animal!" Esteban protested.

"You get to watch, old fellow," Robinson told him, his breath ragged now from desire. "I'll show you how it's done."

Nate and Butch didn't know it, but Bobbie Jean, like some Indian women, carried a "rape knife" on the silver chain around her neck. Its blade was only four inches long, but Jimmy had showed her exactly where to stick it—right between the fourth and fifth ribs. That way it went straight into the heart.

The ropes were free, and Nate grabbed the high collar of her dress, ripping it open.

"Let's have a look at those lovely *chinchonas* of yours," he suggested.

One second longer—that's all Bobbie Jean would have needed to complete her deadly thrust. But Nate caught her wrist before the tip pierced him.

Bobbie Jean cried out when he bent her wrist hard, making her drop the weapon.

"Well now," he said, kicking the knife aside. "*Now* it's going to be even rougher, you little hellcat."

"*Cabrón!*" Esteban snarled from behind them. "*Basura!* Garbage! That is all you are, you scalp-taking monster. Cowardly, murdering garbage!"

Esteban had deliberately intended such serious insults, hoping to distract Nate from his purpose and buy Bobbie Jean a little time. Apparently it worked. Nate turned around to glower at the old Spaniard.

"'Scalp-taking monster'? How many people did you help the King of Spain slaughter to get your land grant, old man? The hell do you know about raising hair, anyway?"

"I know that I despise your very guts for doing it. I killed no one—I was a civil servant in Mexico City. You, however, killed innocent men, women, and children. And skinned them like animals."

"Actually," Nate corrected him, hard-eyed and cruel-mouthed, "we didn't actually kill them all. You see, it doesn't usually kill a person if you scalp them correctly. Not right off, anyway."

Nate stood up. "You pushed it too far, Robles. And you're going to regret it."

Nate crossed to a hidebound storage chest in one corner of the cellar. He returned and held up a curved knife.

Esteban paled. A skinning knife, also favored by scalpers.

"Nate," Bobbie Jean begged, "*no!* Come on back over here, I'll even make it good for you, but please don't!"

But Nate, while smooth and unctuous in public, reverted to his savage nature in secret places like cellars. And the Spaniard had riled him.

"First thing you do to take a scalp properly," he lectured calmly, as if merely explaining a lesson to a class, "is you make your quick outline cut. That loosens the part you need to take. Then, holding the head down with your knee on the neck, you have to get a solid grip and give the entire flap of hair and skin a tremendous tug."

Bobbie Jean was crying openly now as Nate Robinson moved slowly closer to Esteban while he spoke. The curved blade of the knife glinted cruelly in the flickering lantern light.

"The thing is," Nate continued, "just ask any poor devil who has ever survived a scalping what the worst part of it is. They'll all tell you the same thing: It's the sickening noise the scalp makes as it tears loose from the skull. One survivor compared it to the sound of dozens of bubbles popping at once."

Hearing this, Bobbie Jean did indeed almost retch.

"Please, Nate, don't do this," she begged him.

"Sorry, pretty piece, but the old don pushed it, and now he'll stand to account for it. You think I don't know how much he hates me for being a scalper?"

"My only regret," Esteban spat in contempt, "is that I did not tell you to your face long before this."

"No balls, that's why." Nate's eyes were two cold, hard chips of colorless stone. "Well, let me *show* you what it's like to lose your dander, you sanctimonious son of Ferdinand."

"Nate, *NO!*" Bobbie Jean screamed.

Robinson entwined his fingers in Esteban's thick, salt-and-pepper hair, then jerked it tight.

"First the outline cut, like so."

The blade of Nate's knife was only an inch from Esteban's head when a gun spoke its piece. The sound, in the close, brick-lined cellar, was explosive and left Bobbie Jean's ears ringing.

The poorly aimed slug only managed to rip away the point of Nate's bony chin. But the impact shock sent to his brain made him stagger.

Crying out in pain, he turned to see his wife only ten feet away.

"Cynthia! For Christ's sake, what—?"

Just then Cynthia Robinson put three more slugs into him, all in the chest, and he slumped dying to the floor, choking on his own blood.

The newly minted widow—wearing only her linen boudoir wrapper, and still holding her six-shot pinfire revolver—stared at Bobbie Jean.

"Cynthia!" the terrified maid pleaded. "Please, I never—"

"Shush, dear," Cynthia said calmly, dropping the revolver to the floor and crossing to untie the prisoners' ropes. "It was never you, and I knew it all along. It was *that* pig"—she stared at the crumpled heap on the floor—"and his murdering son. I've been playing the drunk to protect myself. They both have big mouths, and I've overheard everything. How they tried to frame Skye Fargo and your brother. How Nate hired Blaze Weston."

"And earlier," Bobbie Jean blurted out, "while you were shopping, Butch murdered Sam Rafferty! Oh, Cynthia, it was so awful seeing Sam lying there that way! They hauled the body out of here a little while ago."

"They intend to frame Skye Fargo for the murder," Esteban chimed in. "That must be their plan. They *must* kill Fargo, just as they intend to kill us, because he knows too much. *Puede ser,* it could be, it was Fargo who told the sheriff."

"At this point," Cynthia said, "I'm afraid Mr. Fargo is on his own. I hope he's as capable as he appears."

"Oh, he knows what he's doing, all right," Bobbie Jean said in a dreamy voice.

Cynthia gave her an odd look, but ignored that.

"As soon as you two are free," she said, "I'm sending a telegram to the governor in Santa Fe. He once practiced law with my father back East. Sunlight is the best disinfectant, and I'm going to shed plenty of light on Nate and Butch Robinson and their Vigilance Committee thugs."

"All right, boys," Butch Robinson announced. "Let's just dump him right here. Ain't like *he* gives a shit."

Josh reined in the team and kicked the brake lever

forward, stopping the canvas-covered freight wagon. They were two hours west of Springer now, and the new day's sun had just risen over the eastern flats.

Besides Josh, whose horse was tied to the tailgate, there were five mounted men, including Butch. All were armed with repeating rifles and packing extra cartridges for a long set-to.

"I don't know, Butch," Josh said doubtfully, glancing all around. "Ain't no place to hide it. It's all open grassland here."

"We don't need to hide it, shit-for-brains. This ain't exactly the Santa Fe Trail, nobody passes this way much. Even if they do, how's anybody gonna know exactly where Fargo murdered Rafferty? We'll be hauling both bodies back, anyhow."

Butch pointed due west. "Straight ahead is river-basin country, boys. Flat, wide-open, nothing but low grass. Fargo should be well into it now. Steve Kitchens is stationed on top Blue Lady Bluff. You can see clear into next week from there. Once Fargo is well past the halfway point of the bottom flats, Steve will flash mirror signals."

Butch's lean, hard features tightened until they stood out like a profile on a chiseled coin.

"Everybody just remember one thing: Fargo is *mine*. Stick to the plan. We run him to ground in the open, then force him into a siege. That's why I had everybody bring so much ammo.

"Kill his horse, but *not* him. He can't be packing that much ammo, and besides, his rifle will heat up too much trying to fend off the wall of lead we'll be tossing at him. Remember, we run him out of ammo, then let him surrender. And then I'm calling the son of a bitch out. Every damn one of you will witness it when I kill the great 'legend' of the West."

"He won't surrender," Josh insisted. "Ain't in him."

"What's his choice once we run him out of lead? All right, so he cheats me by saving the last bullet for himself. That'll ruin my day, but not my week. And he'll still be cold as a basement floor, now won't he?"

"You underestimate him, Butch," Josh warned stubbornly. "Skye Fargo is all grit and a yard wide."

Nobody saw the Remington fly into Butch's fist. But Josh was sure as hell fully aware of that huge bore, staring back at him like a single, unblinking eye.

"What the hell?" Butch demanded. "You and Fargo bunkmates now? Just who the hell's side are you on?"

Josh's shoulders slumped in defeat. "Yours, Butch."

"Then *act* like it, goddammit! And act like you got a set on you, *all* of you! It's six to one, and we're packing over a thousand rounds between us. Skye Fargo is chicken-fixins, that's all. Josh, dammit, toss that corpse off, I said. It ain't exactly got a perfume smell to it."

Sam Rafferty, a good man who gave thirty years of his life to protecting the law-abiding, was dumped from the wagon into the grass like a piece of broken, unwanted furniture.

Despite his glossy cavalry boots, Butch had never been in the Army. But he liked to act like a field commander. He started barking out orders now.

"Every man checks his weapons, then his cinches! Remember: Once the signal comes, we form wide intervals and close in on Fargo. Force him to use up his ammo, but *don't* shoot to kill."

Forty minutes later, a series of bright mirror flashes lit up the horizon northwest of them: Steve Kitchens, signaling from Blue Lady Bluff.

Butch let loose a yelp. "Let's go, boys! Rape the horses and shoot the women!"

When Fargo spotted a series of mirror flashes, northeast of his position, he knew trouble was coming. He drew rein, swung down, knelt to place his fingertips lightly on the ground. Minute vibrations told him his enemy would soon enough be upon him.

His situation was precarious. He was crossing the Canadian river basin, flat grassland.

Oh, for a clay hill right now, Fargo thought. Nothing stopped a bullet like thick clay. No ricochets, no rock dust or chips in your eyes.

But even stuck out here, Fargo knew no ground was ever truly flat. There were always rises and dips, unnoticed above ground level, that gave a man a critical edge against long-range fire.

Fargo splayed himself out, eyeing the terrain from literally ground level. He located a slight depression not too far distant, and led the Ovaro to it.

"All right, old friend," Fargo said as he quickly stripped the saddle, "you been through this before."

Horses seldom laid down unless they were sick or hurt. But Fargo, knowing a breastwork could be mighty handy in open country, had trained the Ovaro to lie on his side when guided by a pull on his neck. Once the stallion was down, Fargo used the saddle as a partial shield for the horse's vital organs.

Dust plumes out ahead were followed by riders materializing out of the horizon's haze. Six, Fargo finally counted, all fanned wide to close the back door on him if he tried to retreat.

Fargo cursed himself for not stocking up on ammo in Santa Fe. He had plenty of loads for his Colt, but no reloads for the Henry. And since his rifle was most crucial now, he would have to husband those sixteen shots wisely.

The riders, probably with spyglasses, had spotted his position and bore down on him at a full charge. That, at least, would work to Fargo's advantage, he figured. The fools had needlessly lathered their horses, and now the mounts would be less adept at cutting and swerving.

There was a rolling crackle of gunfire as the attackers opened fire. Very few shots, from that initial volley, even found their range. Soon enough, however, bullets were thumping near his position nineteen to the dozen.

A round thwacked into Fargo's saddle, and his stallion flinched.

"Steady, boy," Fargo told the Ovaro as he laid the Henry's barrel across his flank.

He had no choice but to fire back. Some of the most daring riders were on the verge of killing his horse.

Fargo expended four quick rounds, scoring no hits but forcing the lead riders back. He recognized Butch Robinson's cavalry boots and snakeskin-banded hat among the pack.

However, the undaunted attackers simply switched tactics, diverting to the flanks and attacking Fargo from both directions. He was forced to expend another precious eight rounds from his Henry, managing to tag one attacker in the leg.

Next the men switched to an Indian-style circling attack. This was truly troublesome, for by staying in fast motion they made poor targets. All they had to do was gradually tighten the noose.

Fargo held off as long as he dared, snapping off a round each time some rider got crazy-brave for a moment and swooped in close enough. But soon he was down to his Colt, and time was working against him.

Fargo knew surrender, even if apparently offered, was not an option. These men, spurred on by Butch Robinson, meant to kill him. Their shot patterns told him they were toying with him at the moment, but that still didn't matter. He was determined, like the elite Sioux Kit Fox warriors, to pin his sash to this very spot—here, on this piece of ground, he would win or die.

A rider veered in, drawing aim on the stallion. At this range Fargo had no chance of hitting the man with his Colt. But he managed to hit the horse and drop it to its front knees. The rider was taken up behind one of his companions.

But that was the Trailsman's last bullet.

A few minutes later, Butch Robinson shouted: "Run up the white flag, Fargo! We'll take you in for a fair trial."

"I'll run my boot up your ass!" Fargo yelled back.

"Make it hot for this mouthpiece, boys!" Butch shouted.

The crackling explosion of gunfire sounded like an ice floe breaking apart. *It's curtains,* Fargo told himself, though even now he felt no fear. Only the determination that he'd be damned if he was going to just hunker down here and die like a pig at slaughter. He'd go out fighting his enemies on his feet like a man.

Even as lead blurred the air around him, Fargo yanked the Arkansas Toothpick from its boot sheath and launched himself to his feet.

"Come on, then, you sniveling weak sisters!" he roared out with the powerful bray of a buffalo bull bellowing. "Skye Fargo never had plans to live forever!"

* * *

No one could move unseen, through so little cover, as could the Apaches.

Earlier that day, from their eagle-eye vantage point in the surrounding high country, Jemez Gray Eyes and his band had begun watching the drama before them unfold all morning.

Curiosity drove them to leave their ponies hobbled and sneak closer on foot—long their preferred way of approaching and fighting an enemy. Now, unnoticed in the confusion of the nearby battle, they crouched only a few hundred yards away. The six of them had once fought off a thirty-man detachment of Mexican regulars, and this group before them posed no threat.

"*Look* at Son of Light!" Jemez said, admiration clear in his tone for the first time as he spoke of this nomadic white man. "Brothers, this is a Fighting-Man!"

This was high praise indeed, to call him by their own name. But even now the fearless white warrior stood boldly in the open, his hair and clothing flapping like lance streamers as bullets fanned past him. Knife in hand, his face and voice defiant, he was actually rushing at his well-armed enemies! And *look* at his war face! Several of the riders were actually backing away in fear.

Courageous and defiant to the very end. He meant to curse his enemies with his dying breath, face-to-face—exactly the code of the Apaches.

"Brothers," Jemez said, shrugging his carbine off his shoulder, "you know me. You know I would let these white devils kill each other and then gladly make water on their bones. But this Son of Light . . . the stories about him are all true. These dogs need six rifles and countless bullets to even face him. *I* am for evening the score!"

"Straight words," agreed Hoyero. "He is a Fighting-Man, a brother."

The rest nodded assent, and the Apaches began moving stealthily forward.

Butch Robinson was laughing so hard he could hardly get the command out of his mouth.

"Cease fire, boys!" he shouted. "Hell, cease fire! Our big hero has finally reached the end of his tether."

Fargo presented a pathetic spectacle, to Butch. *Look at the asshole, standing there with two empty firearms, yet flashing that damn knife—with a half-dozen rifles notched on him!*

"You're deader than a dried herring, Fargo," Butch told him from a sneer. "Toss that pig-sticker away."

"Kiss my ass, Robinson. I'll drop it when you cowards kill me, not before."

Butch shucked out his Remington and blew Fargo's hat off his head.

"I said drop the knife, Fargo!"

"And I said kiss my ass, you spineless, murdering piece of shit."

"T'hell with this, boys!" Butch shouted. "Fill his horse with lead!"

Rifles shifted target, but the only horse to die was Butch's, suddenly shot out from under him. With a bloodcurdling war whoop, the outlaw Apaches rose from the grass as one man, carbines blazing.

The sight of six leather-hard Apache warriors, all armed to the teeth, struck instant panic into the hearts of the vigilantes. They immediately wheeled their horses, trying to escape.

But the savvy Apaches knew a horse was a bigger target than its rider, and they had become excellent marksmen. Within fifteen seconds, every horse had been killed or dropped. The Apaches showed no mercy, slaughtering every man and then bending over each victim to take weapons, money, clothing—anything deemed worthy of stealing.

Butch Robinson, however, they deliberately ignored. He would be left to Son of Light.

His horse had been dropped so suddenly that one of Butch's legs got trapped. While he struggled to free it, one of the Apaches—a Mescalero and the band's leader, Fargo guessed—walked straight up to Fargo.

The Mescalero held a Colt aimed at him—a Colt just like Fargo's, taken off one of the dead men.

Their eyes met and held for a long time.

"Dagote," was all the Apache finally said. And relief washed over Fargo. It was simply the word "hello." But

no Apache ever used that greeting with anyone but a fellow Apache or an admired outsider.

"Dagote," Fargo replied.

The fierce-looking Apache handed Fargo the loaded Colt even as Butch, looking pale as clean sheets, finally freed himself.

Fargo transferred the bullets to his own Colt while the Apaches withdrew about fifty yards. They were waiting with bated breath to see how this would play out.

Butch climbed slowly to his feet, staring at the carnage all around him. He didn't look at all brash now without his bully boys to back him up—and to show off for.

Fargo finished reloading and dropped his Colt back into the holster.

"All right, Butch," he said. "You been wanting your big chance. Now it's here. Let's me and you get to waltzing."

"Fargo, you can't be fool enough to call *me* out?"

"It's past that. You called *me* out a few days back, the first time you insulted me. Now let's put a ribbon on it."

"F-Fargo, you're a fool! Hell, you know how many trophies I've won for my shooting skills? Let's just call it quits now and you ride on outta here, why don't we?"

Fargo shook his head. "I don't care a frog's fat ass about your trophies. Painted targets don't stare back, do they? And those long hours you spend practicing your draw in front of a mirror—how many *mirrors* have ever shot back?"

"Don't push this, Fargo," Butch warned, a fear glint in his eyes. "I can clear this holster before you're half-way out of leather."

Fargo nodded. "Don't mean nothing now. Take a look at your right hand."

Butch did. It trembled like a kitten in a cold rain.

Fargo held his own hand out—so steady a child could have spun a top on it.

"You'll clear first," Fargo agreed almost cheerfully. "But you'll buck your shots. And I won't. All your 'skill' don't amount to a hill of beans now. It takes courage to face a man down, courage you don't have. Now I'm done jawing about it—fill your hand, trick shooter."

In a blur of speed, the Remington was in his fist. And Butch did indeed squeeze off two quick shots, both whistling a whisker wide, before Fargo blew a hole straight through his heart.

As Fargo rode east toward Springer, the Apaches had descended on Butch's corpse like vultures, picking him clean.

Fargo had no idea where Nate Robinson was, or if Sam Rafferty had been able to arrest him on anything yet. But the Trailsman knew one thing for sure—Blaze Weston might well be in Springer by now.

And hellfire was coming with him.

15

For Springer, as for the rest of the grateful New Mexico Territory, several nights passed with no further fiery nightmares spawned by Blaze Weston.

With the damning testimony of Cynthia Robinson, Bobbie Jean and Jimmy Davis, and Esteban Robles, Skye Fargo's name wasn't just cleared—he was declared in newsprint as "the iron backbone of America" and loudly proclaimed a hero. Or as Moonshine Jones aptly put it: "The same damn fools itching to kill you are now lining up to buy your whiskey."

EVER-VIGILANT TRAILSMAN SENDS FEARED ARSONIST PACKING!!! shouted a confident headline in the Springer newspaper.

But Skye Fargo wasn't buying any of this ink-slinger's claptrap. That's why he delayed even longer in reporting to Fort Union to begin his new scouting duties.

It wasn't Fargo's way to leave a job unfinished. Especially a job this important.

Blaze Weston's trail had led straight to Springer, and Fargo had found fresh signs of the man all around the area. But he'd found no trail proving Weston had ever left the region for good.

He's biding his time, Fargo speculated. *Because of that "master plan" of his.*

"Glad to be back in buckskins again, Fargo?" Moonshine asked him as he topped off Fargo's glass.

It was top-shelf bourbon he poured now, not the cheap Indian-burner he'd served Fargo before. This was the fourth night now since the famous "siege at river flats" as the news hawks had dubbed Fargo's gutsy show-down west of Springer.

"Glad? It's like having my real skin back," Fargo assured him. "I wouldn't wrap garbage in them machine-made duds."

"See you've stopped shaving, too. Gonna let that peach fuzz on your face grow into a beard again?"

"Does a bear shit in the woods?"

"Mister, if that bear's big enough," Moonshine assured him, "he can shit any damn place he pleases."

Any damn place he pleases. . . .

Moonshine's harmless joke again put Blaze Weston on Fargo's mind. Seemed like everything did, these days. The hero-hungry press may have buried Blaze Weston for good. But, for Fargo, the New Mexico nightmare wouldn't be over until he saw the arsonist's lifeless body.

It was just past sundown, and the Queen of Sheba was starting to come to life. Fargo had spent the past few pleasure-filled nights bunking with Bobbie Jean, who would soon be moving into a new home with her brother Jimmy. Once the public learned how the Robinsons had tried to frame him, lumber orders had begun pouring in, including some lucrative government contracts.

"New sheriff arrives tomorrow," Moonshine remarked, looking glum. "That means I'll likely have to kick him a percentage. It's technically illegal to run whores in the territory. Old Sam, he didn't care and never took a bribe. I oughta know—I tried to slip him one once. Son of a pup socked me one."

Fargo grinned. "Yeah, I got one of those 'reminder' punches myself. It was the straight-and-narrow path with Sam."

Fargo had been proud to be one of the pallbearers at Sheriff Rafferty's funeral yesterday. The territorial governor himself had shown up, along with an honor guard from Fort Union.

"Cynthia Robinson's headed back East," Moonshine told him. "Told the newspapers she ain't ever even gonna *face* west again much less come back out here."

Fargo nodded, not really paying much attention. Bobbie Jean would be waiting upstairs, ready to ride him to the roundup all night. But even that pleasant prospect wasn't foremost on his mind as he glanced past the batwings at the gathering darkness of the night.

" 'S'matter?" Moonshine asked as he wiped the dust out of a jolt glass with the tail of his shirt. "Something on your mind besides your hat?"

Fargo nodded. "Blaze Weston."

"Aw, hell, Skye! He lit a shuck outta here long ago—no pun. With Nate dead, and the whole thing exposed . . . 'sides, that massacre of Butch and his thugs would put the fear of God in any man."

Any man, *maybe,* Fargo thought. But he had no proof whatsoever that Blaze Weston even belonged to the human species.

"Back in a bit," Fargo said.

As he had several times a night since returning to Springer, Fargo stepped outside and made a slow, observant tour of the town. In and out of each side alley, circling all the large wooden structures.

Again, nothing. No hobnailed boot prints, no prints left by a chipped rear horseshoe.

Could be Moonshine was right—maybe Blaze *had* finally shown the white feather.

Bobbie Jean was waiting for him upstairs, in a pouting mood.

"Some Don Juan *you* are, Skye Fargo," she complained. "Lookit here."

She flumped the sheet back, showing him she was buck naked. Alabaster skin smooth as lotion, with the exciting, dark contrasts of her pointy nipples.

"I been this way two hours waiting on you, getting so randy. . . . Listen! You make me go without it much longer, long-tall, and I'll *have* to join Moonshine's stable of whores just to scratch this itch you started."

"Never let it be said," Fargo replied, tossing his hat onto a chair and unbuckling his gun belt, "that Skye Fargo ever drove a gal to desperate measures."

The night was his time, and this night Blaze waited until even later than he usually struck.

The wind seemed enraged. Around midnight it had begun to pick up with a fury, howling in off the Texas plains in gusts that whipped the landscape into swirling dust storms.

That wind told Blaze his purpose was right, just. Once he fired his kerosene-soaked tinder, that wind would gust like a giant bellows. The whorehouse would catch fire like a hoop skirt, and everyone inside would be cleansed in hellfire.

Skye Fargo included.

It was the time of night sailors called the dog watch— those last, lonely hours before dawn. Blaze had entered town on foot, gliding like a shadow. He knew Fargo was on the prowl lately, but he also knew that even the Trailsman had to sleep.

Fargo had just completed his latest rounds, while Blaze watched from inside an empty hogshead in front of the mercantile, peeking out from under the lid. Fargo would likely turn in now.

As he slipped into the alley beside the Queen of Sheba, Blaze lovingly embraced his folded-up mackinaw. It held the sacred tools of his trade, including the stolen can of kerosene with its cork stopper.

He reached the apron of shadow surrounding the Queen of Sheba, bent almost double by the wind.

The wind sent especially for this night, for this great ceremony.

Outside his warm bed and far from the naked woman curled against him, Skye Fargo heard the wind rise to a warning shriek that startled him awake.

"What?"

His own voice in the silent room. Signboards flapped crazily outside in the gusts, and he could hear grit slapping against the window panes of Bobbie Jean's room.

Fargo's goose tickle was back, like ants racing up and down his spine.

Blaze Weston was nearby, and fiery death was imminent.

"Again, honey?"

Bobbie Jean muttered in her sleep, smiling, as Fargo stirred beside her, sitting up to dress and pull on his boots.

"Honey, my valentine's a little sore," she muttered without waking up.

Fargo strapped on his gun belt and rolled the cylinder

to check his loads. Then he left the room as he had his first time here—he dangled from the window sill and simply dropped.

He landed on his feet in the alley and filled his hand. But a quick check showed this side was clear.

Fargo sneaked around the corner, the sand-laden wind forcing his eyes to slits. All looked clear back here, too.

But when the wind momentarily died down, Fargo breathed through his nostrils, then felt his skin crawl: the strong, pungent stench of kerosene!

Blaze had started with the long side of the building, away from the alley. Carefully, yet quickly and expertly, he placed his piles of tinder along the base of the dry wooden structure, then soaked them and the surrounding wood with kerosene. One quick pass with a burning rope to ignite each pile, and with this wind, the building would be consumed before anyone even realized it was burning.

He had just worked his way around the corner, beginning on the front of the saloon, when a voice boomed out of the darkness.

"Weston! You sick son of a bitch, *I'm* out here, too!"

Fargo! It sounded like he was right behind the building.

No time for fancy work now, Blaze realized. He stood up, and swung the can of kerosene toward the building to splash it good. He cursed when most of the kerosene bounced off and soaked his buckskin shirt.

"Weston, you *hear* me? I'm *always* out here!"

Closer now, and Blaze began to tremble as his hands fumbled to open the piece of oilskin containing his lucifers. No time for the rope, he'd have to just light it and run.

"It's *over,* Weston! Tonight it's over."

Blaze saw a tall form step around the corner, he struck his match on a dry section of board, and a fragment of the burning sulfur broke off and landed on his kerosene-soaked shirt.

Fargo had just curled his finger around the trigger when Blaze literally became one with his name—he erupted in flames.

Within seconds, in that raging wind, his entire body

was aflame, even his wild hair looking like the biblical burning bush.

Fargo, horrified at the sight and smell of a human being incinerated—even *this* one—nonetheless could not tear his eyes away. It was, after all, the old style of justice: eye for an eye, tooth for a tooth.

But then, ice forming in his limbs, Fargo realized: Weston was long past the point where he should have collapsed, writhing in agony.

Instead, he was stalking straight toward Fargo, arms extended for a fiery death hug!

"Jesus!"

Fargo's shocked brain sent a command to his trigger finger, and he planted two quick rounds in the flaming specter's chest.

Still Blaze lumbered forward, his face melting.

"Fargo!" cried that ghastly, ruined voice. "Fargo, I'll take you to hell with me!"

Fargo snapped off the remaining four rounds, two of them to Weston's charred brain.

And still the burning monster was on his feet, charging! In seconds he would be on Fargo.

KA-VOOM! KA-VOOM!

Bobbie Jean emptied both barrels of her sawed-off scattergun, literally shattering the inhuman demon into flaming bits.

For several minutes, both of them just stood there, speechless, staring.

"Woke up and saw both you and your gun belt gone," she told him, her voice quaking at what she still couldn't believe she'd just seen. "Then I heard you out here yelling."

She followed Fargo as he went around the building, pulling out all the volatile tinder and smearing it into the dirt.

"Skye?" she asked. "How could he keep coming at you like that? He was burning alive, and I saw you put six slugs in him!"

Fargo shook his head. "Ain't got the words to explain it, honey, nor the mentality. And I doubt anybody has."

However, he noticed how the wind had died down completely, and how a pre-dawn peacefulness was settling over the town. La Llorona, the Weeping Woman in the wind, would forever raise her plaintive cry across this ancient land of the thunderbird.

But as Skye Fargo stared at the charred, unholy remains before him, he realized: This night, a terrible demon had been destroyed forever. Bobbie Jean, Moonshine, and every living soul in this building would go on living—as would all the souls Blaze Weston would never, *ever* be able to harm again.

"Guess you'll be headed to Fort Union soon, huh?" Bobbie Jean asked him as they headed back upstairs. "Do that scouting job?"

Fargo nodded. But, in truth, he wasn't heading *right* for Fort Union, though Bobbie Jean didn't need to know that. There was a yellow Western Union flimsy stuffed into his pocket, delivered earlier that day. It was from Rosalinda in Chimayo. Just five simple words that meant he'd definitely be returning soon to his pretty rose.

THE SHUTTERS ARE STILL UNLOCKED!

LOOKING FORWARD!

**The following is the opening
section from the next novel in the exciting
Trailsman series from Signet:**

THE TRAILSMAN #282

KANSAS WEAPON WOLVES

*Kansas Territory, 1860—
where parched ground is watered
not by rain, but by the blood of innocents.*

For a town, the City of Kansas wasn't bad, thought the
big man in buckskins as he rode along the main street,
sitting easily in the saddle on the back of the magnificent
black-and-white Ovaro stallion. Skye Fargo preferred
being out on the frontier, far from civilization, but settlements *did* have their advantages.

Fargo was looking at one of them right now.

His lake blue eyes lingered appreciatively on the ripe
curves of a young woman with long, honey-colored hair
as she stood on the driver's box of a big wagon. She was
supervising the loading of crates into the wagon from a
warehouse alongside the Missouri river.

"Let's go!" she called, hurrying the laborers who were

hauling the crates. "There are people starving in Kansas!"

Fargo reined in and rested his hands on the pommel of his saddle, easing his back after the long ride across Missouri from St. Louis. He was on his way to Kansas, so he was interested in the young woman's comment about people starving there.

Fargo knew that a year and a half earlier, a drought had settled down over Kansas Territory that remained unbroken. The lack of rain had dried up the land and ruined crops, but he hadn't heard that things were so bad people were starving.

That was certainly possible, though, he told himself. Some folks referred to the broad expanse of flatland in the middle of the country as the Great American Desert. Fargo knew that wasn't true; he had crossed enough real deserts to know the difference.

But the prairie could be mighty inhospitable when the weather was too dry, as it had been for the past eighteen months. Clearly it was getting worse.

The wagon being loaded in front of the warehouse was only one vehicle in a line of wagons. As Fargo watched, a man came along the line talking to the drivers. He was short, broad, and muscular, with a red face and fair hair under a broad-brimmed black hat. He carried a curled bullwhip and tapped it against his thigh as he walked.

When he reached the wagon where the young woman was, he asked, "About done, Sallie?"

She nodded and said, "Yes, Pa. I'll pull forward as soon as the men are finished."

So they were father and daughter. Fargo could see the resemblance now. And the young woman was the driver of that rig—an unusual job for a female.

Sallie looked like she could handle it, though. She wore boots, a brown canvas divided skirt, a gray woolen shirt, and a buckskin vest. A brown hat hung behind her head by its chin strap.

She also had a cartridge belt strapped around her

waist, with the walnut grips of a revolver jutting up from the holster attached to it. A shotgun lay on the floorboards at her feet. She was ready for trouble if it came calling.

Her father nodded and moved on to the wagons ahead of her in line. They had already been loaded, Fargo saw, and now men were snugging down canvas covers over their cargo.

Fargo had seen enough supply trains to recognize one when he came across it. He had even guided similar trains across the plains on several occasions in his adventurous career as a guide, scout, and trailblazer. He wondered exactly where this one was bound.

He might have stopped and talked to the burly, fair-haired man, who was probably the wagon master, but he was tired and so was the Ovaro. They had been in St. Louis when the message caught up to him, asking him to come to Topeka, Kansas Territory, as soon possible to discuss a business proposition with a man named Henry Coleman.

Fargo didn't know Coleman, but the man had enclosed a hundred-dollar bank note to show that he was serious, and to pay for Fargo's time and trouble. Since Fargo didn't have anything else on his plate at the moment, he had bought some supplies and headed west. Topeka was still a two- to three-day ride beyond the settlement at the junction of the Kansas and Missouri rivers that called itself the City of Kansas.

Heeling the Ovaro into motion, Fargo started past the wagons, intending to find first a hotel and then a saloon. He hadn't gone very far, however, when a commotion erupted behind him.

Fargo reined in again and turned in the saddle to see that a fistfight had broken out between a couple of roughly dressed men. One of the combatants was a driver from the wagon train. The other looked to be a cowboy.

Whatever had provoked the fight was their business and none of his, Fargo told himself. He needed a drink, a hot meal, maybe a few hands of poker to relax, and a good place to sleep. He didn't need to get mixed up in some fracas.

But then the young woman with honey-colored hair jumped down from her wagon and ran toward the fight, and Fargo had to watch and see what was going to happen.

The cowboy had friends, and so did the teamster. The two groups converged to watch the fight, and a lot of hostile stares were exchanged. But not one was throwing any punches yet, except the two men who had started the fight.

Fargo had a good view from atop the Ovaro. He could see over the heads of the men gathered around the brawlers. The two slugged away at each other, raising a small cloud of dust as their feet scuffed back and forth in the street.

Sallie pushed her way through the other men from the wagon train, not shy about using her elbows to make a path. She broke out of the crowd just as the cowboy landed the solidest blow yet, a hard, looping right that caught the teamster on the jaw and knocked him sprawling on his back. A cheer went up from the cowboy's friends.

If it had ended there, that would have been one thing. But the cowboy wasn't willing to let it end. He stepped forward quickly and swung his leg in a brutal kick that sent the toe of his boot crashing into the teamster's ribs. The man on the ground let out a sharp cry of pain.

"Leave him alone!" Sallie yelled as she threw herself at the cowboy's back.

She grabbed him, but he broke loose, spun around, and swung his left arm in a vicious backhand. The blow landed on Sallie's face and sent her stumbling backwards a couple of steps before she fell.

"Damn!" Fargo muttered. He couldn't let that pass.

Turning the Ovaro, he sent the stallion surging toward the crowd. With startled yells, men got out of the way of the big horse. The crowd parted and let Fargo through, and as he reached the circle in which the two men had fought, he swung down from the saddle.

The cowboy was about to rejoin his friends, not paying any further attention to the young woman after he had knocked her down. He stopped, though, when one of the other men said, "Uh-oh, Brinker, looks like trouble comin'."

Brinker turned and glowered at the big, buckskin-clad man approaching him. It was apparent at first glance that Fargo was no teamster. He was lithe and muscular, with thick, dark hair and a close-cropped dark beard. A holstered Colt revolver rode easily on his right hip, and the wooden haft of an Arkansas Toothpick stuck up from a fringed sheath strapped to this right calf. It was obvious that Fargo knew how to use those weapons, too.

"Back off, mister," Brinker said. "This ain't your fight."

"It wasn't," Fargo agreed, "until you knocked down that young woman."

"She shouldn't have jumped me! When she grabbed me I didn't know but what it was another one o' them Holy Joes lookin' for a fight."

Sallie had pushed herself to her knees by now. She stood up the rest of the way and brushed dust from her skirt. "No one from our wagon train is looking for a fight!"

Brinker pointed at the man he had battered down and kicked. "What about him?" he demanded. "He started the ruckus!"

Sallie bent over the man and began helping him to his feet. He held himself awkwardly, probably because that kick might have cracked one of his ribs.

"Is that true, Matt?" Sallie asked him.

"I . . . I don't know what the big galoot's talkin' about, Miss Sallie," the man said, his voice taut with pain. "I was just sittin' on my wagon when this fella came along and said I spit on his boot."

"You did!" Brinker insisted.

"I never did no such thing! You got me mixed up with somebody else, mister."

"It was him," one of the other cowboys said. "We all saw it, didn't we, boys?"

Nods and mutters of agreement came from the men with him.

"I don't care about any of that," Fargo said flatly as he faced Brinker. "You assaulted that young woman. Apologize."

Brinker sneered at him. "Who appointed you the protector of the fair flower of womanhood, hombre?"

Sallie took a step toward Fargo "It's all right, you don't have to defend me, sir. I appreciate it, but it's not necessary."

Fargo turned his head toward her. "I just don't like to see anybody mistreating a lady."

It was at that moment, from the corner of his eye, that he saw Brinker lunge toward him, swinging a big knobby fist.

Fargo's instincts took over, pulling him sharply to the side, so that Brinker's punch missed him for the most part, barely grazing his right ear instead of landing squarely in his face. Fargo struck back, jabbing a right straight ahead. The punch packed plenty of power, despite traveling only a short distance. His fist sunk into Brinker's belly almost to the wrist.

Brinker grunted as breath sour with the stink of raw whiskey gusted out of his mouth. He stumbled forward, but as he did so, his arms went out and wrapped around Fargo in a bear hug that couldn't be avoided. Brinker twisted and drove Fargo back against the side of one of the wagons.

That impact caused Fargo to lose what little air he had been able to trap in his lungs when Brinker grabbed him. He knew he wouldn't be able to hold out for very long unless he could break the grip the cowboy had on him.

He tried to bring a knee up into Brinker's groin, but Brinker twisted at the hips and took the blow on his thigh. Fargo couldn't work an arm loose, so that left him with only one choice.

He lowered his head and butted Brinker in the face as hard as he could.

Brinker howled as the head-butt pulped his nose and

made blood shoot from his nostrils. He let go of Fargo and stumbled backward, lifting both hands to his nose as crimson welled from it and covered the lower half of his face.

Fargo didn't give him time to recover. He waded in, throwing a left to the belly that made Brinker drop his hands again and uncover his face. As soon as Fargo saw that opening, he sent a right uppercut whistling in to land solidly on Brinker's jaw. The cowboy's feet came off the ground and a second later he crashed down in the street on his back.

He didn't move after that, just lay there giving off soft, bubbling moans.

"Get that son of a bitch!" yelled one of Brinker's friends. The group of cowboys started to surge toward Fargo.

A sharp cracking sound stopped them in their tracks.

They must have thought it was gunshot, but Fargo knew better. He wasn't surprised when the burly wagon master he had seen earlier stepped forward, his bullwhip uncoiled now. Like the black snake that was its namesake, the whip hissed and writhed in the dust at the man's feet.

"That's enough!" the man bellowed. "There'll be no more fighting!" He turned toward the young woman. "Sallie, are you all right?"

"I'm fine, Pa," she told him. "But I think Matt here might have a broken rib."

"Is that right, Matt?"

The injured man grimaced as he nodded. "I'm afraid so, Mr. McCabe. It sure hurts when I move or take a breath."

"We'll find a doctor to take a look at you. Reckon you'll be able to handle your team if those ribs are bandaged up tightly enough?"

"Don't know, but I'll sure try."

McCabe slapped him on the shoulder, which made Matt wince again. "Good man," the wagon master boomed. He motioned to one of the other drivers. "Saul, take Matt here and see if you can find a sawbones."

"Yes, sir, Mr. McCabe," the second driver said.

As they moved off down the street, Matt walking gingerly and slowly, McCabe turned to Fargo and said, "I saw what happened, sir. I appreciate you coming to the defense of my daughter."

"I could have handled this trouble myself," Sallie put in.

Fargo smiled. "Like I said, I won't stand for a lady being manhandled."